This is the inaugural book of Kevin Casey's career. After spending most of his young adult life chasing the bright lights of stardom, he was bitten by the writing bug. Casey was a little uncertain but decided to follow his dream of a career in writing and with a little luck, this is the first of many books to come.

To my family and friends,
thank you for pushing me, encouraging me, and always being there for me.
This wouldn't be possible without you.

Kevin Casey

End Game

AUSTIN MACAULEY PUBLISHERS™

LONDON * CAMBRIDGE * NEW YORK * SHARJAH

Ordering Information
Quantity sales: Special discounts are available on quantity purchases by corporations, associations, and others. For details, contact the publisher at the address below.

Publisher's Cataloging-in-Publication data
Casey, Kevin
End Game

ISBN (9781645752622) (Paperback)
ISBN (9781645752615) (Hardback)
ISBN (9781645752639) (ePub e-book)

Library of Congress Control Number: 2021910840

www.austinmacauley.com/us

First Published (2021)
Austin Macauley Publishers LLC
40 Wall Street, 33rd Floor, Suite 3302
New York, NY 10005
USA

mail-usa@austinmacauley.com
+1 (646) 5125767

Chapter 1

"Fold."

"My God, man, grow a set. We're playing for shots, not real money."

"I thought you Irish could drink?"

"We can drink you Italians under the table any day, asshole."

"Except tonight, right?"

"Shut the hell up and deal."

"Okay, okay, first, a toast. Iry, TD, another job well done."

"Boss, you're the one who deserves the toast. Great planning as always."

"Another one bites the dust! Cheers, mate."

Seems like a typical poker game between friends—in fact, this is just our weekly game. We just also happen to be celebrating. We're a team—Tony, John, myself, and Brian in spirit. We've been friends since we were kids; the fact of the matter is we're closer than most brothers. I'd die for both of them and have come close to it several times.

At first, it was just John and me. I couldn't have been more than two when we met. He and his mom had just come over from the Emerald Island when they moved into the same run-down building in the rough part of Brooklyn. Our moms became close friends within a few weeks, and when both got jobs at the same temp agency, we were left with my drunken father, who wasn't afraid to raise his hand at us, even if we didn't deserve it. Ever since we could put two and two together, we knew we could only count on each other.

Like all friends, we've had our fair share of fights, but when push comes to shove, I could always count on him. In our neighborhood, if you didn't have anyone watching your back, you didn't last very long. It wasn't until grade school that I got a full appreciation of that. I got into a scuffle one day, and at the time, I thought it was nothing. Although looking back, I can see that I bit off more than I could chew. Three against one usually is. I got beat down pretty bad that day, taking shots to the face, ribs, and stomach pinned against a wall, and all I can remember seeing was John pushing his way through the spectators with a rock in his hand and molly whopping the guy closest to him in the back of the head.

Granted, he got up insanely fast, and we both got our asses kicked, but that day I realized I had a friend who would jump in a fight, fully knowing we were going to get beat down and not caring. The kid just wanted to help his friend, and from that day, I knew I had a friend for life, no matter what.

Chapter 2

It wasn't until middle school that we met Brian and Tony. More or less, it's where John and Tony met. I was just there, and Brian was just minding his own business. The four of us shared a class, and like all hoodlums, we sat in the back corner, furthest away from the teacher's desk.

It all started innocently enough when John caught Tony trying to copy my paper one day and called him out on it. Tony, being the new kid in class and not wanting to look like a punk, got defensive and told John he'd have problems if he didn't keep to his own business. This, of course, didn't sit well with the hotheaded friend I had come to know. Before they could get out of their chairs, our teacher Mrs. Hamilton shut them up and regained control of her history class. That only delayed the oncoming fight.

Later that same day, when we were just about to make our way home, John saw Tony walking across the street, and it was on. Before I knew it, John was in a dead sprint at him and just started swinging. As I walked across the street to watch, I could see John getting the first few punches in and figured it would be over relatively quickly. A few minutes into it, however, Tony started getting his hits in and had John gasping for air as he threw him to the ground. Instinctively, I moved to intervene. As I got ready to throw a punch, I was sure would put Tony on his ass, I got tackled from behind.

It was Brian. Brian wasn't necessarily a friend of Tony's; he just saw it was about to be two on one. I took a few shots to the ribs before I got my elbow free and promptly put it into his nose. He stumbled back and regained his balance as I got to my feet. As Brian began charging toward me for a second time, I could see John out of the corner of my eye. Tony had him in a headlock and was swinging freely at his head when John grabbed him by the waist and slammed him into the ground shoulder first. When Brian went to tackle me, I was able to get my arms between us and catch him by the shoulders, and when he attempted to pick me up, I was able to thrust my knee into his jaw, knocking him smooth out.

"Let's get the hell outta here, man!" John shouted with a sense of urgency. He knew someone had to have seen us fighting and probably called the police. Even at a young age, we had a bit of a reputation with the authorities. He started to run to the creek we cut through every day on our way home. It ran from our school right up to our street.

"Hold up, man, we can't just leave them here," I shouted at him.

"What the hell do you mean? You're the one who put him on his ass. Let's go," John yelled as he turned back around to run.

Chapter 3

But I couldn't. There was something about those two that I couldn't shake. They were fighters, damn good ones at that. They pretty much earned my respect that day. Tony had already made his way to Brian as I started to walk back to them. When Tony caught a glance of me coming back toward him, he squared and got ready for round two.

"Just get the hell outta here, man," he said.

"Calm down, kid, I'm not going to try anything; I just wanted to see if you guys were okay," I answered.

Tony didn't know whether to believe me or to put his fist through my face. Luckily for me, he chose to believe me. A few minutes had passed before we were able to get Brian to come to. He was a little fuzzy on what had happened, so Tony and I explained everything. Brian looked confused—not by what had happened, mind you, but confused by the fact that I was helping him up.

"So, you knock my ass out and stick around to brag?" he yelled.

"No, man, that's not it at all," I tried to explain. "Yeah, I was the one who knocked you out, but you're the one who attacked me. We don't have any beef between us; I just wanted to know why? Why'd you jump in?"

"Why? Maybe because you and your little bitch friend were about to beat the hell outta him!" he shouted.

"Yeah, you're right. Do you even know him?" I asked.

"What difference does that make? No, I don't, I just didn't wanna see two thugs beat the living shit outta him for no reason," he said, clenching his fists. I couldn't tell if he was trying not to hit me or trying to hide the fact of how bad his jaw was hurting from being slammed into my knee.

"Look, man, I…"

"Brian, my name is Brian."

"Sorry. Brian, I'm sorry I almost dislocated your jaw. To be honest, this was a stupid fight, to begin with. John's always been a bit of a hothead," I explained.

"Yeah, you should probably get him in check before he gets you into a situation you won't get out of," Brian shot back in a sarcastic tone.

"Good advice; I'm Zack, by the way," I said, extending my hand. I was kind of shocked when he put his out to meet mine.

"How about you, man?" I said, turning my attention to Tony. "Are you all right?"

"Just bumps and bruises," he said, dusting himself off. "I've been hit harder by my sister. My name's Tony."

"Well, fellas, no hard feeling?" I asked, not really expecting them to just forget about everything, but to my surprise, they looked at each other, shook their heads, and then turned back to me to say "No."

"All right then, see you guys around," I said, turning away to head home. I remember thinking how odd it felt to be in a fight and walking away without having to worry about being jumped. Don't ask me how I knew; I just did.

"Hey, Zack," I heard just as I had gotten to the creek bed. I couldn't tell which one had yelled, but once I turned around, I saw it was Tony.

"Yeah?" I answered.

"Tell the Iry not to cry like a little girl when Italy wins tomorrow," he said with a half-smile. If there was anything more important to John, it was the Irish national soccer team, which just happened to play Italy tomorrow. He would've killed me if I were to talk bad about his team.

"Will do, bro, will do," I said. He didn't have to know I was lying, although I'm pretty sure he did.

Chapter 4

The street lights had just started turning on when I walked to my building, and John was sitting on the steps waiting for me.

"Zack, where the hell have you been?" he asked, sounding like a frightened mother looking for her children.

"Calm down, Iry, I was talking to Tony and Brian."

"Tony and Brian? The two punks from the park?" he questioned as he started to yell, "What did you have to say to them? Better yet, why would you say anything at all?" I could tell he was getting angrier with each passing word.

"Relax, kid; it wasn't anything bad. I told them that it was a stupid fight that got outta hand."

"You didn't owe them shit. I don't understand why you would even say anything," John interrupted.

"John, calm your ass down." Now, I was yelling. "Look, man, it's no big deal. I helped them up, and honestly, they're good guys. You might have more in common with them than you think."

"Like what? What could we have in common?" he asked. He had this look on his face that wasn't confusion, but he didn't understand what I was saying.

"You remember when you first moved here? We could barely walk, and when my drunken ass father came at one of us, the other would help. Whether it was cleaning up the cuts or running to get the neighbor, we had each other's backs. Same as those two—hell, Brian was just passing by and jumped in," I explained. The more I talked, the more John seemed to understand what I was saying.

A few days had gone by, and once everyone's temper had a chance to go down, we all met up in the field behind our school with a soccer ball. The four of us just stood there for a few minutes, looking at each other until I finally spoke up.

"Okay, guys, I'll go first. I'm Zack Brown."

"John O'Malley. Everyone calls me Iry."

"Tony DiSalvo. You can call me TD."

"Brian Wilkerson—Bdub, if you want."

"See, that wasn't so bad. Let's play some soccer," I said as I threw the ball out on to the field. As we played, we bonded and started to become friends. I could tell then that we would be a tight group of friends for many years to come.

How we got into this line of work is another story. We're the best, though; however, being the best puts a huge target on our backs, and we all knew that.

Chapter 5

"All right, boys, last hand," Tony said, checking his watch. "Gotta meet a girl about a thing if you know what I mean."

"Yeah, we all know what you mean, jackass," I replied.

"You know this one's name, or are you just gonna hump your way across the city until you find her?" John asked.

"For your information, this one found me," Tony answered.

"All right, all right, c'mon guys, last hand. Tony will forget what she looks like if he doesn't leave soon," I added. I started to shuffle up the cards when a voice with a heavy Russian accent came from just outside the door.

"Deal me in?"

As soon as we heard it, the mood around the table went from fun and games between friends to animosity. We knew it wasn't a request; it was more of a demand. It was our boss, Seri Sokolov, a Russian immigrant who came over with his family some 30 years ago. His father ran one of the most notorious crime families in Russia. Once the Russian authorities started cracking down on his father's involvement in some unsolved murders, they had no choice but to immigrate to New York and set up shop. Seri senior, or simply Senior, as I called him, built the most successful operations on the East Coast. When Senior died, his son took over the business, and some might say he's worse than his father. When Senior ran things, he at least showed mercy; Seri, on the other hand, would shoot you twice then drop you off a building just because he was bored. There's nothing Seri wouldn't do to get what he wanted, and unfortunately for us, we worked for him now.

Chapter 6

It didn't always use to be like this. Before Senior died, life was easier, maybe one or two jobs a month. Ever since Seri took over, we've been on call 24 hours a day, and we knew this wasn't a social visit. Seri had been planning something big for a while now, I could tell by how he was acting. He wasn't his usual sadistic self. Normally, he'd just let us do our thing and not worry about it, but lately, he was being careful. He was always a shoot first and make up the story later kind of guy, but now he was always checking on us and reminding us to be careful and to make sure we were basically invisible. I knew he wanted something as soon as I heard his raspy voice. He would never just show up unless he was desperate.

"To what do we owe the displeasure of your sorry ass being here?" Tony asked as I started to deal the cards across the table.

"What? A guy can't drop in on his employees to see how everything is going?" Seri responded.

"What do you want, Seri?" I asked, putting my cards down. I was a little insulted that he didn't just come out and say it.

Seri was quiet. He took a peek at his cards then looked around the table at all of us.

"Bet's to you," I said to John.

"Raise," he said. We all called the bet then I dealt the *flop* cards.

The bet checked all around the table, and then I flipped over the *turn* card. Once the 7 of hearts showed, Seri's face lit up.

"Raise a hundred," he said, tossing money on the table. We all pulled out money and called the bet, and then I revealed the *river* card.

Again, the bet checked around the table before Seri smiled and said, "Straight, 7 high," and started counting the money on the table. It was a good hand, but three of us didn't give a damn about the hand. We wanted to know why he was here.

"Well then, down to business," he said when he realized we were all staring at him. "I have a job for you."

"We just finished a job not four hours ago," Tony said.

"Yes, and it was a job well done, but you forget who's in charge here," Seri answered. "This isn't going to be a normal job; it's going to be difficult."

"How difficult?" I asked.

"I want you to take out Paul Natano."

"I knew it! You sorry sack of shit, I knew you wouldn't let that go. You have an agreement!" John was outraged and rightfully so. Natano was the head of the family that, Seri believed, murdered his father. He was alone in that belief.

Chapter 7

Three years ago, Senior and Paul's father, Phillip, came to an agreement. They had been at war since I was in school; actually, Senior is the one who got me into this, and I brought my team. I became very close to Senior. He was more of a father to me than my dad was, which is why Seri had so much resentment toward me.

It wasn't until Phillip became ill that he reached out to Senior for peace talks. Seri was furious when Senior cooperated. He thought his father should destroy the Natanos and take over their operation, not show weakness and agree to peace. After all, in Seri's mind, it wasn't just the Natanos they had to worry about; he thought everyone was gunning to be top dog. Senior wanted to destroy Natano's operation, but he also knew that nature would take its course, and when Phillip passed, his operation would wither and die as well. Seri, on the other hand, was too short-sighted to see that. The one thing that stopped Senior from killing Phillip was that he knew that it would start a war based on revenge and that war would kill his son and maybe his grandchildren.

Believe it or not, Senior was a family man. His family meant more to him than power, more than money. So, he started talking with Phillip, started trying to come to some sort of agreement that would stop the bloodshed. After six months of talking, and not to mention six months of conflict between Seri and his father, Senior and Phillip finally came to a truce. Both of their sons were present when they shook hands, and they both knew that their fathers expected them to uphold this truce even after they were gone. Seri wanted to shoot both of them right then and there, and Paul felt the same way, but neither had the balls to stand up to their father.

Three months later, Phillip died due to heart failure. I was at the funeral to pay my respect on Senior's behalf. He wanted to go himself but felt someone's emotions would've taken over, and he might not have come back.

Two days after Natano was laid to rest, Senior was shot. The first bullet entered his back just under the right shoulder, piercing his lung and exiting out his chest. The second hit him in the center of his back, lodging into his spine, which probably would've left him paralyzed. The shooter, knowing that, finished him off by putting one into his skull from point-blank range.

Seri refused to believe that it was anyone else but Natano, but I knew Paul's father. He had his bad sides, but when he gave his word, he stood by it. Even if he hated you, his word was his bond, and he expected the same from anyone he did business with. That made it hard for me to believe that he wouldn't expect his son to do the same, but Seri was convinced. He swore up and down that he'd seek revenge, and rumor had it, that he'd taken a shot or two at it.

Senior's death hit me hard. I made it my mission to find out who pulled the trigger and deliver a little street justice. I lost count of how many punches I threw, or bones I broke trying to get someone, anyone to talk. Every thug I could find told me the same thing. That Paul wouldn't dare cross his father even if he was dead. He had more respect for him than that.

I was obsessed with trying to find out who shot him. I ran the scenario in my head over and over until I finally used a contact I had paid off at the NYPD.

Chapter 8

Officer Stevens was a small structured man, barely a hundred pounds soaking wet. He was the only police officer who has ever come close to catching us. We had just taken out a hitman from Brazil—a brutal, ruthless killer who got off on torturing his victims, a psychopath with no sense of pain or mercy. He was hired simply to provide protection for Senior's old lady, and she was a peach. She never met a man who didn't drool over her, and this time was no different. Of course, Senior warned him that if he looked at her the wrong way, he'd be dead in that same minute, which he just laughed off like it was a bad joke. The Brazilian made a few attempts, as expected, but he was never successful. Finally, his ego couldn't take the rejection and decided to take matters into his own hands.

She was found raped, strangled, and her hands bound behind her back with her right middle finger missing, the psycho's signature. Before she was even cold, John, Tony, and I were on the streets, loaded and hunting him down. It wasn't long until a member of his inner circle told us where we could find him—after being "roughly persuaded," of course.

We pulled up to a dive bar that was notorious as the meeting place for low lives. John and Tony walked around to the back door that led into an alley, and I walked into the front door and saw him sitting at the end of the bar, taking tequila shots two at a time.

"We need to talk," I said as I grabbed his shoulder.

"So, pull up a stool," he said, jerking away from me. "Two more, sweetheart."

"I don't think you heard me," I said, twisting his are behind his back and pulling him away from the bar. He struggled as I moved him through the back of the bar and out the door where John and Tony were waiting.

"What the fuck are you doing?" he shouted as I pushed him into the side of the building.

"You fucked up, man," John said.

"What are you talking about?"

"Wanna tell us where you've been tonight? Where Senior's lady is?" Tony asked.

"What about that stupid bitch?" the drunken hit man answered.

"What did you do?" I asked.

"That little slut wanted to act like she didn't want me, and I got tired of asking nicely, so I just took it."

"You know you aren't leaving this alley alive, right?"

"You think the three of you have the balls to take me on? Let's dance, then," he said as he lunged at John and landed a punch on his jaw.

Drunk or not, he put up a hell of a fight that grabbed the attention of passersby, who naturally called the cops. The Brazilian got off some punishing blows, breaking John's nose, dislocating my shoulder, and somehow managed to put a bullet in Tony's leg. Finally, John was able to get a rope around his neck, and as he struggled for every breath, Tony took an iron pipe to his knees, shattering them both. When he fell to what remained of his knees, I took my knife and severed his middle finger, just like he'd done to Senior's love, and once I had fully cut it off, John finished the job by snapping his neck in half.

Chapter 9

As the Brazilian lay motionless on the ground, the three of us heard the sirens of the single squad car the police had sent. After all, it was a bar fight in a back alley in Brooklyn, not a downtown bank heist. We left the Brazilian where he had died and moved down the alley toward the river, which, we thought, would've been overlooked by any cop when Officer Stevens came around the corner with his weapon drawn.

"Freeze, assholes!" he shouted just as we approached the opening in the alley that no doubt was our escape plan. Stevens' hands were shaking as we turned to see who was trying to stop us.

"Who the hell do you think you are?" Tony asked, shifting his weight off his wounded leg.

"You have no idea what you just walked into, kid," John added.

"Guys, guys," I interrupted, "take it easy. What's your name?"

"Jerry Stevens. Officer Jerry Stevens and you're under arrest," he answered.

"Okay, calm down. Let's just take it easy; you don't wanna do anything you'll regret," I said.

"I wouldn't regret killing you dirtbags," Stevens shot back without missing a beat.

He obviously knew what he was doing even though he clearly had never fired his .9mm at anyone. Luckily, his finger never reached the trigger.

"I said freeze!" he shouted a second time when he noticed that we were still backing toward the openings that lead to our eventual freedom.

"Stevens, look down there. You see that body?" I asked as I took a step toward the officer. "That man is responsible for numerous unsolved murders in your city."

"I don't care who he is. All I need to know is that there is a dead body, and you three were running away from it. That makes you suspects," he said with his gun fixed on my chest, but his eyes were bouncing all over the place.

"Hey, focus on me," I said, trying to figure out how we were going to get out of this.

"Tell me," I continued. "How's everything going?"

"How's everything going? What the hell kinda question is that?" he yelled. Stevens looked confused, and that was our chance. As he tried to process what I had asked him and figure out what I was up to, he lowered his weapon just enough.

That split second of confusion was all John and Tony needed to swing around and grab him by both arms. Stevens struggled all the way to the ground as Tony knocked his gun away, and John unhooked his radio. Tears in his eyes, he started begging for his life as I picked up his gun and removed the clip and the one in the chamber.

"As far as the NYPD is concerned, you saw three men leaving the scene. You fought with one and lost your radio, then emptied your magazine, trying to stop them. As far as you're concerned, we own you now," I said as I stood up, reaching into my pocket to grab a stack of crisp, newly printed 100-dollar bills and tossed them on to his chest. When they landed, Stevens let out a sigh like he had been holding his breath, waiting to be shot. Before he could get back to his feet, we were gone.

We had used Stevens for help as far as information was needed—like if someone was under surveillance or on the Organized Crime radar. Little things we needed to know in order to stay invisible and off the radar. When I called to find out what New York's finest had uncovered in their investigation into Senior's death, he confirmed my suspicions. Not one witness, detective, or anyone else for that matter could put Natano at the scene. If anything, they had an alibi for him.

Paul Natano may have been a lot of things, but he wouldn't go back on a promise to his father. Seri, on the other hand, didn't seem to share that point of view on that subject. This is why we were so upset. In this life, if you don't have your word, you have nothing, and by the sound of it, Seri had nothing.

Chapter 10

"Why the hell do you want us to take out Paul?" Tony asked.

"Why wouldn't I?" Seri started. "We're rivals and have been since I can remember. Not to mention that piece of shit killed my father."

I looked up and made eye contact with John. He was the only one I had shared my suspicions with regarding Seri and his father's death. He had the same "*Yeah, right*" expression on his face that I did.

"Look, you three are on *my* payroll, and if you don't want me to put a price on your heads, you will do this," Seri said, pointing his finger across the table. I could see John start to say something before I cut him off.

"Can I talk to you in private? Boys, play another hand or two, we'll be right back."

"You got it, boss," John said with frustration in his voice.

I lead Seri down the dusky hallway that came out to the back porch that had a couple of chairs and a cooler of beer where the guys and I would sit and drink the night away.

"What the hell are you thinking? You want us to take out the one guy you told your father you'd leave alone?" I asked, not knowing exactly how I felt. Anger, confusion, disgust—I had all these different emotions, and it was taking a minute to process it all. It was all I could do not to just start swinging at him right then and there. If it wasn't for the gun tucked into his waistline, I probably would have.

"I knew you wouldn't let this go. You still think he's responsible for your father's death, don't you?" I don't know why I was asking because I already knew the answer, and I knew he would sidestep the question.

"Last time I checked, you worked for me, not the other way around. Which means I say 'jump,' you say 'how high,'" he answered, pushing his chest out as if he was sizing me up. "You're going to do this," he continued, "or I will break every bone in your body. Now you and your boys need to start doing what you do best. You've got two weeks, better get to it," he said, turning his back to leave.

"What do we get?" I asked. That stopped him dead in his tracks. Seri turned around slowly, trying to hide his disgust at the fact I would even ask.

"What do *you* get?" he repeated. "On top of what I already pay you? You're already getting a very generous salary," he continued, anger rising in his voice.

"That's true. However, this is a slightly different job," I said as the wheels in my head started to turn. I had been wanting out for a while now, and unfortunately, there were only three ways out—prison, turning state, or death. I don't plan on dying anytime soon, I'm no snitch, and we're too good to get caught. This was my chance to get out clean or at least as cleanly as possible, and I had to take it. Another one may never come.

Chapter 11

"What do you want?" Seri hesitantly asked. "More money, women, cars, jewels, what?" He was clenching his right fist, the one he was imagining putting through my face. I made sure to know where both his hands were, not to mention the gun I noticed earlier. I was sure he had a second one somewhere on him. I started scanning every inch of the porch, looking for possible weapons in case Seri decided to act on the rage he was feeling. For what I was about to ask, I knew I could be in for a fight.

Seri may have been a "white-collar" kind of boss, but he was no pushover. He could handle himself very well. Being around the business for as long as he had, he became a very competent fighter. He's probably seen more people get their ass kicked than any four people put together, so I had to be careful.

"Well, are you going to answer me? Or are you going to keep looking for something to swing at me?" he said with a little sarcastic smile. As I said, he was good.

"All right, Seri, here are my terms. On top of what you're going to pay us, I want out," I said, never disengaging from eye contact, partially to gauge his reaction and to make sure I could react if he made any sudden movements.

"You what?" Seri was furious. He took this as a personal insult, and that was an unforgivable sin in his eyes. "You want out? Are you fucking kidding me? Nobody walks away from this, especially in my family."

"Look, the way I see it, you're asking us to kill the one person you swore you'd leave alone, which will start a war that I want no part of. So, you have two choices, I'll do this last job for you, and you let me out. Or I don't, and you have to take care of it yourself, and I disappear anyway. It's up to you," I said as I opened one of my favorite beers and sat back on one of the chairs. I could only imagine what was going through his mind. The look in his eyes and the sound of his teeth grinding told me just how mad he was. He couldn't believe I was asking this.

Chapter 12

"You want out?" he repeated, still in shock.

"You can repeat it all you want; it's not going to change," I shot back. "Do we have a deal?"

"How do I know you won't turn state? It'd be easier to just kill you now," he said, pulling back his black leather jacket to show me the gun he had tucked into his waist.

"You're right; it probably would be. But that would leave you with two problems. One, Natano would be left alive and kicking," I started.

"A problem that's easily fixable," Seri interrupted. "And the second would be?"

"If you were to shoot me right now, there isn't a snowball's chance you'd get away from the two in there," I said, pointing at the door. "They would make you their next target, and you know exactly what they are capable of," I finished as I took a long drink from my beer, never breaking eye contact.

"You ask me something of this magnitude, and then you insult me by sitting and drinking a beer?" Seri said. "Do you even fathom what you're asking?"

He was getting angrier with each word that was spitting out of his Vodka-soaked mouth. Honestly, to his credit, I hadn't fully thought this through. There were so many outside factors that could contribute to this, but I didn't care. Hell, at this point, I was intentionally trying to push every single one of his buttons. I wanted him mad, to the point where he'd agree solely out of his frustration to prove that he was still the alpha in the family.

"The choice is yours, Seri," I said with a smirk on my face. This wasn't the first game of mental chess I had played with him. I knew what I was doing, and to an extent, what he was thinking.

"Fine," he said reluctantly. "When you prove that Natano is dead, you're done. But you listen to me, you little fuck. If I ever, and I mean ever, get word of you in my town, I will not hesitate to destroy every person you have ever cared about. Then I will find you and empty a clip into your head. Understood?" he threatened, standing a few feet from me with his right index finger extended.

The veins in his neck were bulging out so out far that I could almost follow them past his reciting hairline. By the time he had finished yelling his threat, Tony and John had made their way to the patio, looking like two older brothers who heard the smallest being bullied, ready to fight.

"So, we have a deal?" I asked one more time. I wanted him to say he agreed out loud, this time with people around to hear it. I know it doesn't make much sense to trust a mob boss for any reason, but it would just make me feel better if I had his word. Just as I was about to ask again, he finally said it.

"Yes, Zack, we have a deal," he said with a look of disgust on his face.

Something about the way he gave in made me a little suspicious. *Why did he agree so easily? Why didn't he take a swing, a shot, something?* Thoughts were racing through my mind faster than I could process that I just decided to dismiss them as occupational paranoia. After all, I just got a feared mobster to agree to let me out of the life *and* still pay me.

He could've easily said he wouldn't pay me, and I would've accepted that in a heartbeat. We both would've gotten what we wanted—I would've been out, and his rival would've been decomposing somewhere, waiting for someone to stumble upon the remains. Whatever the case, I wasn't putting much thought into it.

I started to stand as Seri went for the doorway before stopping between Tony and John. He looked back over his shoulder and said, "Don't fuck this up," then stormed off.

Chapter 13

"What the hell was that about?" Tony asked. "We're not actually going to take this job, are we?"

"Zack, c'mon, we said we'd leave this one alone," John added.

"In a technical sense, it was Senior that said *he'd* leave it alone," I said. "We're doing our job—nothing more, nothing less."

I looked at both of them. Tony had the same expression he always gets when we accept a job. It's a mixture of excitement, nervousness, and fear, although he'd never admit it. When I looked at John, his expression was very different. He was shocked that I took this job, and he had every right to be. I still couldn't believe that I accepted it, but I didn't have time to worry about that now. I was on a schedule, and I had work to do.

"Look, guys, I took the job," I started. "Before you guys start on me, I already know how wrong it is, but I'm the one that has to deal with it, not you."

"Would we at least be getting a shit ton of money for it?" John asked, trying to justify it.

"The usual," I answered.

"I'm sorry, but did you just say the usual?" Tony jumped in. "Boss, for this, we should be getting at least double."

"I'm with him. What's in it for us?"

"Our contracts," I said with a little bit of excitement that I couldn't hide.

"Our what?" they both said in sync.

"That's right, boys. We do this job, and we're done."

"What the hell are you talking about?" John asked.

"Look, I don't know about you guys, but I have wanted to get out for a while now," I explained. "After everything we went through with Brian, I started thinking about life after the job. Guys, we deserve a retirement plan just like everyone else."

"Boss, you've got to stop blaming yourself for Brian."

"Actually, I don't," I said. "It was my fucking fault, and we all know that. We've made peace with it, but it doesn't mean I don't think about it every day, and I'll be damned if I let that happen to you guys."

The guys just sat there for a few minutes. I could tell they knew how serious I was, but I could also see that they were remembering our friend, the one that always told us to go out with the guns blazing, even in a losing battle.

"Let me be clear, guys—if you don't want in on this, just say the word, walk away, and that's that. No hard feelings, no resentment, nothing. But that means you stay under Seri's thumb," I explained. "So, you guys in?"

There was a pause between the three of us that seemed to last for hours. Tony stared at the ground with his arms crossed over his chest as John made his way to the refrigerator and grabbed three more beers. He handed one to each of us when he got back and sat down, drank half of his in one swig, and smiled.

"I've had your back since we were three; no way am I stopping now."

I smiled and looked up at Tony, who hadn't looked up yet. I didn't want to rush him; I was asking a lot. After a few minutes, he let out a big sigh, followed by a short, loud yell.

"Hell, someone's gotta cover John's ass—I'm in."

"All right, boys, we got work to do," I said with a smile.

"Cheers."

Chapter 14

Lightening was creeping up in the distance. We sat out on the patio for a while, just watching the storm roll into the city through the clearing that looked out over the Hudson River. There was something calming about watching a storm light up the skyline of New York. Every time one came rumbling through, the three of us would sit out there and just watch; we were mesmerized by them, and none of us knew why. These were the times we could just sit and clear our minds without having to come clean about what we've actually done.

"How much time do we have?" Tony asked between lightning strikes.

"Two weeks," I answered. "And this isn't going to be a regular job, guys, we've got to do some serious planning."

"You win understatement of the year," John remarked. I could tell that this wasn't sitting well with him.

"Boss, he's got at least two guys with him wherever he goes. Not to mention that paranoid psycho constantly has his head on a swivel."

"Yeah, you're probably right," I said. The more we talked about it out loud, the more I realized how difficult this was going to be.

"Okay, boys, I gotta run," Tony reminded us.

"Yeah, get out of here, man, go have some fun," I said as he got up and started making himself presentable.

"You got any plans tonight, John?"

"Nah, boss, I got nothing going on."

"Sounds about right," I joked. "Let's go see if we can't find some company for tonight. Tony, be back here tomorrow morning, we gotta get to work on this."

"You got it, boss," he shouted back as the door shut behind him.

Normally I would've put us on lockdown, especially given what we were about to attempt, but for that same reason, I figured one night couldn't hurt.

Chapter 15

When Seri made it back to his million-dollar penthouse, his girl, Natalya, was waiting for him with nothing but a red silk robe on and his favorite bottle of vodka in hand.

"They take job, yes?" she said with a Russian accent as thick as Seri. Natalya was about five-foot-nine with blonde hair stopped just passed her shoulders, legs that seemed to go on for days, a tight little ass and amazing breasts, a woman that was every bit as dangerous as she was beautiful. She had been around the family ever since I could remember, and rumor had it, Seri's receding hairline wasn't the only thing he got from his father. We called her the Viper. The bitch was cold; there was nothing she wouldn't do to get what she wanted. There was talk that she would even pull Seri's strings from time to time.

"Yes, honey, they're going to do it," he replied.

"You're going to pay them?" she continued to pry. The worst kept secret in the world was that she absolutely despised us.

"I was going to," he said, taking a shot. "Then that bastard, Zack, said something to make me reconsider. He asked to get out."

"Out?" Natalya asked, as shocked as Seri was when he had first heard the request. "He had the audacity to ask to get out? After everything you have done for him?"

"Yes. That's on top of what he wants me to pay him?" Seri answered.

"Do you think he would rat?"

"I don't know. That's a big risk, one which I'm not sure if I can afford to take. That asshole thinks that he's got me by the short and curlies. He knows how bad I want Natano taken care of. He also knows that they will probably get away with it. Nobody gets out of my business, especially while they're still breathing!" Seri said, just as agitated as when he'd left the back patio. He downed his vodka and slung the glass through the window that overlooked the park across the street.

As he stared aimlessly out the shattered window, clenching both his hands as if he were holding on for dear life, Natalya slowly removed his wet, black, leather jacket and tossed it to the couch. She ran her hands up his back and began massaging his shoulders as the wheels in her head started spinning.

"Baby, baby, baby, relax. I have an idea," she whispered.

"What's that?"

"You agree…"

"Agree!" Seri interrupted.

"Yes, agree, only in words. Add your own stipulations. Make them use a driver, so you know they aren't going to skip out. Once they do what they were hired to do, have them meet you at the river banks where you'll pay them and part ways."

"Yeah, then what?" Seri asked eagerly.

Natalya said nothing. She just grabbed him by the arms, spun him around, and started kissing every inch of his face and neck. As his eyes began to roll back in pleasure, she stopped. Seri's eyes promptly opened with confusion and frustration.

"Then what?" he repeated.

Natalya then flashed her beautiful smile, the same one she'd shown off many times to get what she wanted. She slid her hands down his sides to the pistol tucked away in his waistband and said, "Then you get creative. Make sure he doesn't leave under his own power."

Seri's face filled with excitement as he realized what he never thought of. He processed the idea for a few seconds before turning back to his love.

"Of course! Why didn't I think of that?" he asked, almost dumbfounded.

"Because you were enraged and couldn't think clearly. It happens when people when they get older," she simply replied.

"That's why I love you," Seri said, leaning in for a kiss.

"I thought this is why you loved me," she said as she dropped to her knees.

"Let's go to bed," Seri said after a few minutes. "I'll call that piece of shit tomorrow."

Chapter 16

The next morning, I woke up around noon to the sound of Tony walking in with lunch. John wasn't far behind him with a case of beer and a bottle of Jameson Irish Whiskey.

"Breakfast of champions," I said, walking out of my room.

"Well, I figured since you guys struck out last night, I'd bring something that you have a chance with," Tony said.

"You're such a douche after you get laid, you know that?" I said, chuckling.

"Have you put any thought into this?" John asked as he cracked open the bottle and poured three shots of our favorite whiskey.

"Well then, straight to business," Tony said, a little disappointed that he wouldn't get to tell us about his conquest from the night before.

"Some, yeah," I said, not looking up. "The hardest part is going to be the planning. And this can't be our normal *'wham bam'* kinda job. We have to be careful."

"You aren't lying," Tony said as he took a bite out of a slice of pizza from the best hole in the wall joints in the city. "So, let's get to it."

"Natano is going to put up a hell of a fight," John said, reaching for a slice.

"We'll have to act fast. We're not going to have a large window, especially if he sees us coming. Hell, he'll probably take a few shots at us if we aren't careful," I explained.

"What if we go at him when he's mobile? Like driving?" Tony asked.

"That's one way. It'd have to be perfect, though. Shoot the driver, car crashes, and then we get closer to finish him off. A car crash isn't a death sentence," John explained.

"That's true. Plus, as careful as he is, it's a possibility he probably has bulletproof windows," I added. "We need to know his routine, where he eats, drinks, that kinda crap."

"Hey, do we still have Stevens on the payroll?" Tony asked as he finished off his beer.

"Oh yeah, that little moron doesn't have the balls to turn on us. He knows he wouldn't last long if he did. Why?" I answered.

"Well, it seems to me that a major crime boss like Natano might be under police surveillance at some point," Tony explained.

"I'll make the call," I said. My phone started ringing as I reached for it.

"Hmm, that's strange," John commented.

Chapter 17

When I saw that the caller ID said Seri, my stomach started to get a little uneasy.

"Brown," I answered with a stern voice.

"It's Seri; how are my favorite little puppets?" he asked.

"That is the last time you will ever refer to us at puppets, understood?" I shot back. Nothing pisses me off more than being blatantly disrespected by a punk-ass low life. "What do you want?"

"We need to talk about the finer details of our latest agreement," he said. I could almost smell the strong stench of Stoli on his breath.

"What do you mean, *finer details*?" I asked.

"If I'm going to let you fuckers walk after this, then I need to know that you're actually going to do it," he answered.

"Why, Seri, I'm offended. Don't you trust us?" I said with nothing but sarcasm in my voice.

"Trust you? That's funny, kid. You three are the shadiest people on this godforsaken planet, and you want me to just trust you? I'm not my father. My trust is earned, not given," Seri said with growing anger in his voice.

"You're not half the man Senior was, may he rest in peace. What *details* do you want to discuss?" I asked.

"Look, dipshit, I'm risking a lot here. So, if I say we're changing things up, that's what's going to happen. I'm making you go off-book," he shot back. I was surprised by his reaction. I was expecting him to explode on me and to get into a screaming match. Although I could hear the hatred toward me, something was different. He almost seemed calm.

"How do you mean, *off-book?*"

"I want someone I can trust with you guys so that I don't have to stress about you turning ghost," he started. "I'm sending a driver."

"Now, why the hell would we agree to that?" I asked. It wasn't our style to use a driver, or have anyone with us for that matter.

"Because I'm letting you walk. So, if I say you're using a driver, then dammit you're using a driver!" Seri shouted. "You don't have to change any of your plans. He's just picking you up, escorting you to the job, then delivering you to me, where I pay you, and we go our separate ways."

"All right, fine. Who are you picking?"

"Joey."

"You've got to be fucking kidding me. Joey? You're sending us with your nephew?" I asked. I was feeling how Seri must've felt when I asked for our contract. I was completely blindsided.

Joey was a good enough kid. He didn't really have much common sense, which his uncle took full advantage of. This wasn't the first time Seri tried to use him to accomplish his own goals. Seri's sister had asked him to do his best to keep Joey out of that life, so Seri just used him to run a few "errands" every now and then. Joey was a people pleaser, and he would never say no to his sadistic uncle.

"What's wrong with Joey? He's family and one of the few people I trust," Seri said.

"Well, for one, he doesn't know his ass from a hole in the ground. Two, this could be really dangerous; you'd really risk Joey's health over Natano?" I said, trying to change his mind while reiterating the fact a "stray" bullet might hit Joey.

"Watch your fucking mouth. You will not disrespect my nephew. I'm not asking you, I'm telling you. Who knows, he might even surprise you. Oh, and by the way, anything happens to him, it'll be your ass!" he shouted as he hung up.

Chapter 18

"Well, fuck," I said as I hung up and tossed my phone on the table.

"What's up, boss?" John asked.

"Seri's making us go off-book," I replied.

"What do you mean, off-book?" Tony asked.

"It's still up to us how to proceed, but he's just making us take Joey as a driver," I answered.

"Joey? That guy is a fucking idiot," John said after another shot.

"That's what I said, but, as he put it, he's letting us walk, so he calls the shots on this one," I said, reaching for my next beer.

"I don't like this," Tony said. "I don't trust him, especially since he's risking his own blood to keep an eye on us."

"What is Joey supposed to do?" John asked as he opened himself another beer.

"He's supposed to drive us to the job, we do what we do best, then he's to take us to the river where we meet with Seri, he pays us, and we walk away," I said, looking at both of them. "John, I want you to make sure he doesn't fuck us on this."

"I'll watch him like a hawk," he said.

"I mean, if he goes to the bathroom, I want you whipping his ass," I reiterated.

"White on rice, boss, you got it."

"Good. In the meantime, let's go pay a visit to our favorite beat cop," I said, reaching for my .9mm and one last swig of my beer.

Chapter 19

Stevens patrolled out of the 54th precinct in northern Midtown, which just happened to be the same part of town that Natano ran his operation from. We rarely made visits to the precinct, simply because it made us nervous, but this was a special occasion.

"Hey, Stevens, your carjacking suspect in interrogation one."

"Thanks, Ryan."

"Oh, before you go in there, Captain wants to see you ASAP."

"Oh, that's just what I need. Did he seem mad?"

"Surprisingly, no."

Captain Todd was a very interesting man. He always seemed to put himself on New York's most strange and gruesome murders. He enjoyed the challenge of matching wits with the psychos of the world. Even more interesting, he always seemed to be the lead investigator on the "jobs" that my team and I carried out. Rumor had it we were his *Moby Dick*.

"You wanted to see me, Captain?" Stevens said, peering into his office.

"Yeah, Stevens, get in here," Todd answered. "You did a hell of a job cracking that GTA case."

"Thank you, sir," Stevens said, rubbing his sweaty palms together. "But, I haven't closed it yet."

"Minor details, your suspect had the keys on him plus the blood of the victim all over his hands. All you have to do now is just get the bastard to confess," the captain answered, leaning back in his chair and sipping his coffee.

"Hopefully won't take too long," Stevens said. "Is that all you needed, sir?"

"As you know, Ryan's partner is transferring to Miami…" Todd started.

"Yes, sir," Stevens said with a knot in his stomach.

"How would you like to take his spot?"

"You mean as detective?" Stevens eagerly replied.

"No, I mean his parking spot," Todd responded with a half-smile. "Yes, as detective. I'm promoting you, effective immediately."

"Thank you so much, sir! This is what I've been working for my whole career; you will not regret this," Stevens said as he stood to shake his mentor's hand. As he did, Ryan walked in, smiling and with open arms to hug his new partner.

"Congrats, kid," Ryan said as they sat back down in front of their captain.

"Well, boys, ready for your first assignment as partners?" he said, handing them both copies of a file.

"Yes, sir," the detectives said one after the other. As soon as Stevens opened the file, his stomach began to churn, and his hands started shaking. He did everything he could to hide his nervousness from his new partner and his captain.

Chapter 20

"I'm going to assume that you both know who Seri Sokolov is, correct?" Todd asked as the two detectives started reading the files.

"Yeah, he's a second-generation scum bag, runs most of the Northeast Coast," Ryan answered.

"That's correct. I've spent half my career trying to put that bastard behind bars," Todd said, tightening his grip on his *World's Greatest Cop* coffee mug. "However, I've come to realize that he's extremely cautious and rarely does his own dirty work."

"Who's the guy?" Ryan asked.

"That is a surveillance photo, taken off a cell phone, of Sokolov's 'supposed' hitman," Todd said, leaning forward in his chair.

"*Supposed?*" Ryan questioned.

"Gentleman, we're not exactly following procedure. We're working on a hunch. Nobody outside this room is to know about this, understood?" Todd asked. Both Stevens and Ryan shook their heads but didn't say a word.

"Good," Todd started. "The man in the photo is Zack Brown."

As soon as Todd finished his sentence, Stevens' heart began to race. He started to breathe heavier and heavier as if he were having an asthma attack.

"Brown has been involved with the family since before Seri took over. I've been trying to catch him for years. He's the only one who can lead us to Sokolov," Todd said in a hushed tone.

"If he's been around for so long, then how come we don't have a record of him?" Stevens finally and shakily chimed in.

"That's just it! This guy is so damn good that he's never been caught. Hell, he's probably never been a suspect," Todd said as he slammed his fist into his desk.

"C'mon, sir, nobody is that good," Ryan said, flipping through the pages of the file. "I mean at most, all we have is him talking to Sokolov. That's not exactly a smoking gun."

"True. That's where you two come in. I want you guys to look under every stone there is, talk top every low life that's in or associated with Sokolov's crew. Find the link between Brown and the unsolved in that file," Todd said, tapping the papers.

"With all due respect, sir, what if he really had nothing to do with all this?" Stevens asked with a cracking voice. "This is all circumstantial at best."

"There is something that connects him to those deaths. I'm absolutely sure. Now you two go find it!" Todd shouted, rising out of his chair.

"I've never seen him like that," Ryan said as he shut the door behind him. Ryan was a 15-year veteran of the force and the best detective the precinct had to offer. He'd given his best years and a marriage to the city he loved. All that seemed to be left was retirement, but like every good cop, he claimed he wasn't ready for it. Stevens made the sixth detective that he trained.

"He's very determined. Which means if we don't find Brown, our lives will become hell, so let's get to it."

"What about my GTA case?"

"Oh yeah, you have the guy in custody, right? Crack him in an hour, I'm going to grab lunch, and I'll meet you back here," Ryan said, pulling on his jacket. "I'll even bring you back some, rookie."

"Thank you, sir," Stevens said as he turned and headed toward the interrogation rooms.

Chapter 21

As he walked down the hallway, his nerves got the best of him. He started thinking to himself how important his new assignment was to his captain and what would happen to him if anyone were to find out that he had helped Brown by providing some very valuable information. *Could I really get through this without being found out? Even if I do get discovered, I did what I did out of fear for my life. That's got to mean something, right?*

As each step passed, Stevens felt more and more nauseous. He had no choice but to dart into the men's room and vomit like a frat boy the day after a bender. He crashed into the first stall he saw and began to empty his guts into the toilet. When he felt like there was nothing left in his churning stomach, he flushed and staggered to the middle of the three sinks to rinse his mouth and wash his face.

"Damn, I'm glad there wasn't anyone in here to see that," he said as he peered into the mirror, still trying to catch his breath.

"Oh, I wouldn't say that."

As soon as the words left my mouth, Stevens jumped and spun as quickly as he could only to see the three of us standing behind him and locking the door.

"You all right, buddy? You don't look so hot," John said, leaning against the back wall.

"What the hell are you guys doing here!? This is a police station. It's like holy water to a demon for you," Stevens said, basically whispering.

"We came to check up on you, Stevens. How long has it been since we just sat and chatted?" Tony asked, putting his arm over Stevens' shoulders.

"Chatted? You're fucking kidding me, right? You guys don't 'chat,' you manipulate until you get what you want. Why are you here?" Stevens asked again with his voice rising.

"Easy buddy, wouldn't want any brothers in blue to wonder who you're yelling at in the crapper now, would we?" I said, taking a few steps away from the door. "But you are right. We're not here for a social visit."

"No shit, Zack. You shouldn't be here at all," Stevens said, pushing himself out from Tony's arm.

"Why the hell not? Outside of the stale doughnuts and crappy coffee, it's cozy. I kinda like it," John interrupted.

"Because, shithead, the captain just gave me the job of proving that you're Sokolov's hitman. On top of that, he wants you to flip on him," Stevens continued.

"Right, a patrolman who's gonna run point on a major crime investigation? That'll be the day," John said from his position behind me.

"It's not patrolman anymore, asswipe, it's detective," Stevens shot back with a little bit of pride.

"Detective Stevens? That does have a nice ring to it," Tony said.

"Yeah, and my first job is to find you and get you to turn on your boss," he said, which made the three of us laugh.

"Good old Captain Todd," I said with a grin.

"What's that supposed to mean?" Stevens asked.

"Well, Detective, as I'm sure you're already aware, the good captain has been after me for quite some time now," I explained. "And, unfortunately for him, he's yet to realize that, for one, he's practically chasing a ghost, and for two, even by some miracle he does catch me, he'll have to kill me."

"How do you know he's been after you? This could all be recent," Stevens couldn't help but ask.

"I learned at a very young age that if I was going to get away with anything, I had better know who was chasing me," I said.

"How do you know I won't turn you in?" the new detective asked.

"Stevens, if you had the balls to turn us in, you could never prove our involvement in anything relating to Seri or his business," I said, staring him down.

"I know, I know," Stevens said, looking away. "All we have is circumstantial at best, but Todd is determined to take you guys down."

"So, it would seem. Lucky for us, ain't it, boys?" I said, turning to look at them.

"What do you mean? What are you planning?" Stevens questioned, going back to his hushed tone.

"We're planning a job, and at the end of this job, we walk," Tony answered.

"You walk? Just like that? Why would your boss let you guys walk?" Even little piss ant cops like Stevens knew that you don't just leave the mob.

"That's how bad our boss wants this taken care of. He's willing to recognize our years of service and let us move to Florida to play golf to get it," John said.

"Which brings us to why we're here," I started. "We need all the information you have on Paul Natano."

Chapter 22

"Natano? Your last job is to take out your employer's rival? There is no way that you could do that and not leave a trail," Stevens said.

"Maybe you're right. But by the time you hear about it, we'll be long gone," I answered. "Now, I want Natano's file in the morning."

"Or what?" Stevens said. His promotion had clearly given him a confidence boost.

"Well, let's think about this, there are three of us in here with you, and the door is locked behind us. Now you can be a good little detective and get me that file, or…" I paused and just looked at him.

The new detective wasn't sure what was about to happen. His guard was up, however, and so were his arms. They were crossed over his chest as if he were trying to show us that he wasn't intimidated.

I took that opportunity to step toward him; Stevens went to step away, but his nerves had gotten to him and slowed his reaction time. I grabbed his right elbow and spun him down to the ground. As he fell, he reached for his gun, but he was too late. I was able to get my hands on it before he had the wherewithal to reach for it. Panic set in as he lay on his stomach with his own service weapon pressed against the base of his skull.

"Or you can keep trying to act like a badass and end up in a shallow grave in Central Park," I said as Stevens struggled to get free.

"Okay, okay. I'll get it for you," he said.

"See, that wasn't so hard, was it?" I said as I let go of his arm and dropped his gun next to him.

"But dammit, this is the last time," he started to say as he got up. When he turned around, there was nobody in the room with him. We had already left.

Stevens came out of the men's room, looking frantically in every direction for the slightest clue on which way we went.

"Stevens, you all right? You were in there forever," another officer asked.

"Yeah," Stevens said, still a little shaken. "I gotta lay off the egg and cheese omelets."

Chapter 23

We made our way through the station toward the front door, trying to draw as little attention as possible. A couple of *"Afternoon Officers"* later, we were outside, heading west on 54th street through the area of midtown Manhattan.

We weren't out of the woods yet. Cops were known to park up and down the few blocks surrounding the precinct, and with Todd now leading a crusade against us, we didn't know how many dogs were chasing our scent. Not to mention, we didn't wanna be spotted by Natano's crew.

After about ten blocks, we jumped into a cab that looked to be waiting on a well-dressed businessman who was walking out of a building on the north side of the street.

"Hey, that's my cab!" he shouted as John and Tony made their way into the back of the well-maintained Crown Vic.

"Well, that's a damn shame," I said, pushing the man aside to jump in. "On the plus side, this is New York. Another one will be here soon, I'm sure of it. Have a nice day." I shut the door to the cab as the businessman continued to scream obscenities and flip us off.

"Where to?" the driver said in a Jamaican accent.

"Brooklyn."

"Brooklyn is kinda big, Mon, any particular spot?"

"Woodwork, 583 Vanderbilt," John said.

The whole ride lasted right around 20 minutes, and the three of us said nothing despite the Jamaican's multiple attempts to start small talk.

"You guys are real quiet," he said as he stopped outside of O'Malley's, which happened to be one of our favorite bars in the city.

"A bit of free advice, Rasta, be careful who you talk to in a cab. You might learn something you want nothing to do with," I said as I flashed the gun tucked in my jacket.

The Jamaican didn't seem to be intimidated by it. He didn't even seem surprised by it. Knowing how New York can be, I assumed that it wasn't the first gun he'd seen.

"Forget you saw us," I said as I dropped a 100-dollar bill into the front seat and turned to walk into the bar.

I spotted the boys sitting at basically the last table in the back, where Tony had already ordered a round for the table.

"Thank you, sweetheart," I said as I sat and quickly reached for my drink. "Can we go ahead and order three more?"

"You got it, sugar," she replied. "Rough day at the office?"

"You have no idea," I answered as she flashed her pretty smile and left to put in our order.

"Boss, you sure we can still trust Officer Dipstick?" John asked. "I mean, his sole purpose now is to bring us in. And you know Todd isn't going to let him do anything else."

"I hate to say it, but I think Johnny might be right on this one. I mean, Todd's been chasing us since he worked the beat," Tony added. "And now we're using his own hunting dog to get us intel? Can we trust it'll be right?"

"I've been thinking the same thing. As of right now, we have to work under the assumption that Todd knows about us using Stevens. If we get the file, we'll check it for bugs and see if everything makes sense," I said, still planning it out in my head.

"And if we don't get the file?" Tony asked. I honestly didn't know what to say. I took another drink and looked up at them.

"I guess we'll cross that bridge when we come to it. If Stevens doesn't come through for us, we assume he's flipped; however, if we do get it, that doesn't mean he hasn't said anything either."

"Worse come to worse, we'll have to add two bodies to our total," John said.

"There's always a silver lining for you, isn't there?" Tony asked with a smile.

Chapter 24

The three of us sat in silence for the next several minutes. Looking around, I saw what you'd see in any bar in the early afternoon. A couple of old-timers reminiscing about the "good ol' days," a few kids playing pool trying to impress the waitress they had no chance with, and the bartender staring at the TV watching the highlights from the night before. As our waitress walked up to the bar with a Styrofoam cup to make her a soda, John watched her every move.

"Damn, she is fine as hell."

"You wouldn't know what to do with it, Iry," Tony said as he checked her out for himself.

As she turned away from the bar, she locked eyes with us and made her way to our table. The boys weren't wrong; she was a very attractive girl. She was right around five-foot-six with brown hair that went down to the middle of her back. I could tell she worked out at least twice a week. She had tight toned calves and a hot pink Nike wristband around her forearm, holding a zebra-printed bar tool in place. She stopped at the top of our table, took a sip of her soda, and sized the three of us up.

"I've seen you guys in here before."

"Oh yeah?" John said, taking a drink. "See anything you like?"

"A few things, actually. I've heard some rumors about the line of work you are in," she said, taking a seat in the extra chair.

That comment caught us off guard. I knocked on the table twice, making sure the boys knew not to say anything while I tried to figure out what she thought she knew.

"And where exactly did you hear these rumors?" I asked.

"In a bar, people talk. At first, it was just a few whispers, but then I started asking around," she explained.

"And what kinda rumors are you hearing exactly?" I continued to question.

"That you should be in jail or dead," she said, not even looking away. "It's kinda hot."

"Excuse me?"

"I have this thing for *bad boys,* and ever since I heard that, I can't help but fantasize about you," she said as she leaned in closer and began rubbing my leg under the table.

"So, you're just looking for a good time?" Tony interjected.

"With this one, yes," she answered, still leaning on me. "Veronica, by the way."

"Zack."

"My shift just ended," she started to say as she grabbed my hand and started to write her number. "Give me a call sometime. Trust me; it'll be amazing," she added with a seductive little smile and turned to leave.

I watched her walk away as best I could without letting her know I was watching her. I'm pretty sure she knew, though. As she turned into the kitchen, she pulled out her phone and sent a text.

He's got the number. Be ready.

Before I could take another drink, Tony and John burst into a roar of laughter. I sat my drink down and waited for the comments that weren't far behind.

"What the fuck was that? You could've fucked her right here on this table." John said, still laughing.

"How do you luck into these girls, boss?" Tony added. "You gonna call her?"

"Does a bear shit in the woods?" I asked.

"Not if he's in a zoo," Tony replied.

"Yes, smartass, of course I am going to call her," I said, chuckling. "All that shit aside, you guys hungry? Let's get some food."

Chapter 25

"I'm getting antsy," Seri said as he walked out of the bathroom into his walk-in closet that could easily have been used as a spare bedroom. "I haven't heard from that bastard in almost a week."

"Darling, you shouldn't worry."

"Shouldn't worry?" Seri interrupted. "Are you fucking kidding me? Zack is supposed to be working for me, doing something that would expand my empire and make me the most powerful man in the northeast. And you want me to not worry?"

"All I'm saying is that you know how Brown works, you've been around him since you were kids, and you yourself have admitted that he's the best. If you're that worried, call him. Or get Joey to go over there," Natalya said with a calming tone. There was something about the way she phrased things that always calmed Seri down. Almost like a mother talking to an upset child.

"Yeah, you're right. I need to call both him and Joey," Seri replied in a much calmer voice.

He walked across the room, looking out the window to get a feel on what the weather was like. It was November, but uncharacteristically warm for New York. He picked up his phone; as he started to dial, he paused.

"Love you, my sweet," he said, looking at his girl who was lying on the bed, stomach down, flipping through the pages of the latest *Cosmopolitan*.

"I know, sweetheart, I know," she replied, not bothering to look up. Seri simply sighed, finished dialing, and then started moving toward the living room for a little more privacy.

Chapter 26

Joey wasn't your typical "mob thug." He didn't even carry a gun, although he did know how to use one. He mostly kept his nose clean; however, when his uncle called, no matter how big the favor, Joey was eager to help.

"Hey, Seri," he said with a little hesitation.

"How are you, Joe?" Seri asked.

"Oh, you know me, just keeping busy."

"Yeah, I know how that feels. Listen, I need your help."

"With what?" Joey asked.

"You remember Zack, right?"

"Of course, we've had a few run-ins. He's a sick son of a bitch. He's beat me down a few times," Joey replied.

"How would you like to get even?"

"All right, you've got my attention."

"He's planning a job for me. I need you to be my spy, and let me know what he's planning."

"How would I do that? There's no way he'd let me in on the job," Joey asked, not knowing what to think.

"I've already taken care of that. He knows you're coming. You're actually going to be his driver on this one," Seri explained. "I need you over there. Today."

"No problem, I'll be there later today."

"Good. Oh, and Joe, watch yourself, he's a sneaky little fuck," Seri said as he hung up.

Seri tossed his phone onto the coffee table and made his way to the liquor cabinet. He picked up a bottle of Stoli and poured it over the usual four ice cubes. He sat down on his plush leather couch and smiled.

"It's just a matter of time. Natano will be dead, and I, *me, Seri Sokolov*, will run the East Coast," he said to no one. Seri was proud of himself for getting all the pieces together. He finished his drink, got up, and looked into the decorative mirror.

"You've outdone yourself. You've got Brown getting ready to take out your rival, and then you're putting a bullet in his head. Two people you hate the most will die within hours of each other. Two birds, one stone."

Chapter 27

The sun was just beginning to set, turning the skyline of NYC into a beautiful blood orange. Stevens was sitting at his desk, flipping through the file Todd had given him, and tucked underneath his keyboard, was the file on Natano that he wasn't sure what to do with.

"You still here, Stevens?"

"Yeah, been going through the file you gave me, just seeing what I could see."

"Making me proud already, but I did just give it to you. Go on home—you, me, and Ryan will take a look at it tomorrow," the captain said.

"Yes, sir, enjoy the rest of your night," Stevens said, gathering his things, including the file on Natano.

As Stevens made his way out of the station, Todd headed back to his office. He sat behind his desk, grabbed two glasses, and poured three fingers of single malt scotch into both.

"How'd it go?"

"He took the file," Todd said, taking a sip.

"And how do you know for sure he's the one who took it from the archives?"

"The archives are locked, and since we went digital, you have to use an access card to get in. He's the only one who accessed that room," Todd said as he stood to stare out the window.

"You just promoted him; there's no way he would be dumb enough to use his own access card to get the file."

"You're exactly right, he's good, very observant, and he's picked up a few tricks. He used mine," Todd said, not turning around.

"*Yours?* How the hell did he get your card?"

"I'm not sure he's the one that got it," Todd said as he refilled the two glasses. "I sent it down to the lab, and the only two prints on it were mine and a set of unknowns."

"You didn't really think you'd find his prints, did you? He probably used gloves."

"More than likely, but what bugs me is the unknown prints on my card match the prints in the file I just assigned him. Pretty big coincidence, don't you think?" Todd asked.

"What do you want me to do?"

Todd let out a sigh and sat back into his leather chair. He stared at his glass for a minute before finishing his drink.

"Follow him for now. If he's doing what I suspect, he's probably going to the drop point right now. Take photos but do not approach, understood?"

"Yes, sir."

"Oh, and Ryan, be careful, Brown and his team are good, believe me," Todd said as he scratched his left shoulder.

"Understood," Ryan said as he shut the door behind him.

Chapter 28

Todd sat in silence as he finished his second drink. After putting the glasses away and heading for the door, his phone started to ring. Usually, he wouldn't answer, figuring it wasn't anything that couldn't wait until the morning, and knowing his wife would call his cell. Wanting another swing of his scotch, he figured *what the hell.*

"This is Todd," he said, reaching for his bottle.

"Hello, Captain." Todd was shocked to hear my voice on the other end of the line.

"Brown? You've got balls calling me."

"Yeah, that's been said. How are you, Greg?"

"Let's cut the bull shit, Zack, what do you want?"

"Just called to see how you're doing. It's been a while since we talked."

"It's kind of hard to have social interactions with the scumbag that I'm chasing."

"It's a shame. We used to be so close."

"Until you decided to be a low-level enforcer for a dirtbag."

"If memory serves, you weren't exactly a straight arrow."

"You never answered my question, Brown, what do you want?"

"How's the shoulder?"

"The one you put a bullet through?" Todd shouted. "It's fine."

I didn't say anything for a few moments. I was getting under his skin. Todd wasn't an easy man to rattle unless you know what buttons to push.

"Why the sudden interest in my shoulder?" Todd finally asked.

"Saw you rubbing it."

Todd froze. His instinct was to hit the floor and get away from the windows, but all he did was wait. He tensed up like he was waiting for a bullet to pierce through his back.

"Relax, Greg."

"You gave Stevens my card? Got him access to the file you need? What do you want with it?"

"You're assuming a lot."

"Where are you, Zacky?"

"Turn around."

I hung up and could see Todd drop his phone and spin around to the window. I simply stared at him and then waved. I could see him shouting what I could only assume wasn't very nice things. Then he turned and rushed out of his office. I didn't panic—by the time he got over here, all he would find was a cell phone that could not be traced, and a bottle of *Glenmorangie,* the same scotch he'd been drinking all night. He had nothing.

Chapter 29

Todd bolted through the station, knocking over chairs, tipping over tables, and pushing past other officers.

"You three with me, now! Hurry up, let's go!" he shouted as he burst through the front door. He didn't even slow down as he sprinted across the street, forcing cars to slam on their breaks and blast their horns.

Todd raced around the building across from the station toward the fire escape, with the three officers on his heels. As they reached the top of the stairs, Todd slowed and waited for the others to catch up. Using his hands, he instructed two of the officers to the left and the other to back him up as they went right. Guns drawn, they rushed on to the roof.

Each pair going their assigned ways, they circled the building meeting on the side closest to the station, finding nothing but the bottle of scotch and cell phone I had left. Todd holstered his weapon as he knelt down to get a better look.

"Wanna tell us what this is about, sir?"

"We're hunting a fugitive. Get Ryan and Stevens back to the station, now! I don't care what they're doing, get them here," Todd said as he stood up, phone and bottle in hand. "After that, get back to your normal shifts."

When Todd got back to the station, he went straight to his office and waited for his detectives to arrive. He sat the phone and bottle on his desk and just stared at them. He knew what he had to do, but he didn't know just how to do it. Ryan was the first to show up, looking like crap.

"You wanted to see me, sir?" Ryan asked as he poked his head through the door.

"Get in here and shut the door."

"What's going on, sir?"

"Brown was here," Captain said.

"Here, like at the station?" Ryan said as he sat down.

"At this station, yes. He called me about two hours ago from the roof of that building," he replied, pointing over his shoulder. "I found these up there."

"Were you guys sharing a drink?"

"Nope, the bottle was for me. It's my favorite one," Todd said, pulling out the bottle that they had drank from earlier.

"There's no way he could've seen that from the rooftop. How'd he know that?" Ryan asked, looking at the building across the street.

"One problem at a time," Todd said. "Did you get anything yet?"

"Unfortunately, yes," Ryan said, looking almost grim. "I went to the address on file, the one you suspect Brown works out of."

"Mike, I *know* he works—possibly even lives—there. I'm assuming after tonight, you know it too," the captain interrupted.

"Right—anyways, I didn't see Brown, but I did see this," Ryan said, handing him a file. "It's Stevens walking up to the door and dropping 'something' into the mail slot."

Todd didn't seem surprised to hear that his suspicions were true. He'd probably been preparing for this since he decided to promote Stevens.

"What do you want to do?" Ryan asked.

"I want to hear what he has to say for himself, first. Hell, who knows, he might be on to something."

Chapter 30

Stevens arrived at the station about an hour later to find his partner and his captain sitting in silence. Both men looked upset; however, Ryan had a look on his face that made Stevens instantly nervous.

"What's going on, guys?"

"Stevens, take a seat, we need to talk," Todd said as he stared a hole through his newest detective.

"What's this about, sir?"

Todd didn't answer. Instead, he sat back and let Ryan take the lead.

"Look, Stevens, I like you. You've got a shit ton of potential, but there's something off about you," Ryan said as he repositioned himself on the opposite side of the desk.

Stevens' heart began to race, his breathing increased rapidly, and his palms began to sweat. This was the moment he'd feared for years. He knew he'd been found out, but to what extent. In the back of his mind, he always knew this day was coming, so he did everything he could think of to cover his tracks.

"How do you mean, off?" he finally replied.

"Well, let's put it this way," Todd said. "I went down to the archives tonight just out of curiosity, seeing as how my keycard was used to open the door and all, and just happened to notice that a few of the boxes were jumbled up."

"Jumbled, sir?"

"Out of order, not the way they should have been. So naturally, I took a closer look. There was a file missing. Everything the department had on Paul Natano, to be exact," Todd began to explain. "Now I've been after Brown for a while and have always seemed to be one step behind him. Now I just assumed that there was a leak in my department. Imagine my surprise when I found out that the file that I can't seem to find just happens to be the one on Brown's rival boss."

The more Todd spoke, the more nervous Stevens became. He tried frantically to control his breathing.

"I don't see what this has to do with me," he managed to spit out.

"Well, my key card was the only one used to access that room this afternoon. Now I know it wasn't me, so I dusted the card for prints and found two sets—mine and a set of unknowns," Todd explained.

"An unknown? Now I'm really confused. If I understand you correctly, you're accusing me of taking a file using your keycard? Not only do I have my own card, but an unknown set of prints was also found? My prints are in the system," Stevens said confidently.

"You're right. Any cop worth a damn would've worn gloves, which brings me to my next point. The unknowns on my card match the set in the Brown file I gave you yesterday," Todd said with frustration in his voice.

"So the prints on your card match the supposed Brown prints? And you drag my ass down here for what? Pin it on me? This is bullshit!" Stevens said as he slammed his hand on the desk.

"Bullshit, huh? Then what the hell is this?" Ryan asked as he tossed a photo on the desk in front of him.

"Looks like a surveillance photo," Stevens answered.

"Look closer," Ryan said. "It's you putting the Natano file in the mail slot of Brown's house."

"That's a stretch. You've got a guy in a black jacket, and you assume it's me?" Stevens asked.

"Well, there's that, plus the fact that Brown told us."

Chapter 31

Stevens' face went as white as the edges of the photo that lay on the desk in front of him. He was completely blindsided.

"Brown called *here*?" he asked as his voice cracked.

"That's right," Todd answered. "I'll give you the benefit of the doubt right now. Brown basically confirmed my suspicion about you. Now I'm giving you a chance to come clean and save yourself from jail time. Maybe even your job."

Stevens took a moment to think about everything. He thought about how much he loved his job, but on top of that, he thought of his family. He would be risking every single person he ever cared about if he were to come clean. Was it worth the risk? Would his family be safer with him behind bars? Or in Witness Protection?

"All right, it's true, but if you want to know what I know, I need you to promise that my family will be put into WitPro," Stevens said. He was just like any other criminal. Deny everything until confronted with the evidence you can't dispute.

"You have my word," Todd answered. He couldn't help but feel a little bit of excitement. He has finally gotten reliable information that Brown didn't know about.

"How long have you been helping him?" Ryan shouted.

"A few years, usually just for information."

"Do you realize how fucked you are?" Ryan asked as he moved closer to him. "We could charge you as an accessory to murder."

"Look, I know there is nothing that makes this sound right, but it was either do what he said or die. I did what I had to do to survive, and sir, I swear I never did anything to compromise your investigation into him," Stevens said as he pushed away from Ryan.

"You've fucked us, Stevens. I can't believe you'd betray the badge like this," Ryan said.

"Ryan, take five, go get some coffee," Todd finally said. As the heated detective stormed out of the office, Todd folded his hands over the photograph that was still on the desk. "He's right, you know? You've completely screwed our investigation."

Hearing how disappointed his boss was, weighed heavily on Stevens. He had so much respect for Todd. He had really been the only one to show any faith in him.

"However, I really believe that you didn't do anything to tip off Brown. So you're going to help finish this case. You're going to tell me everything that you've learned not only about Brown's operation, but also the job he's working on right now. After that, we'll decide what to do with you."

Stevens sat in silence with so many thoughts rushing through his mind. He rubbed his eyes with his clammy hands before making eye contact with Todd.

"Okay, listen up. He works fast."

Chapter 32

Tony was the first one up, as he usually was. It was shaping up to be a dark, gloomy day. A cold front had blown through overnight, and you could hear echoes of thunder in the distance. As Tony walked from his room to the kitchen to make his famous buttered toast, he noticed a gift had been left for us.

"Well, look at this," he said to his shadow. "Didn't think he'd actually come through this time."

As he headed back toward the kitchen, opening the envelope to examine its contents, John came stumbling through his door and down the hallway.

"You look like shit," Tony said as John made his way to the table.

"Of course I look like shit. Do you know how much we drank last night?"

"I feel fine," Tony said with a half-smile.

"Yeah, well, you also don't share a wall with the love birds either," John said, reaching for a piece of toast. "God, I can't wait until he humps this one out of his system."

"You don't like her either?"

"She's a sweetheart, don't get me wrong, but something about her just seems off."

"Yeah, like how she is always with us. She basically lives with us. Have you noticed how focused she gets when Seri calls? Like she wants to be a part of the conversation. Or how she hangs around when we try to get work done," Tony said, voicing his own concerns.

"For starters. Just the way she studies Zacky like he's a fucking science experiment, or how she *knew* who we were. Either she is an obsessed crime buff and wants a life in this world…"

"Or?" Tony asked impatiently.

John took a deep breath and carefully looked over his shoulders. "Or she was sent."

"Sent? Get outta here; you're fucking paranoid, man," Tony said, shaking his head.

"Am I? Think about it for a second. She could've been sent by Natano. If he's as good as he says he is, he'd know how to get to us. Or Todd? He's been after us basically his whole career. Or hell, Seri could've sent her," John explained.

"Seri isn't that stupid," I said as I walked through the doorway toward the fridge. Both John and Tony's eyes watched my every move. They weren't scared—more surprised that I was able to sneak up on them.

"Now, why don't the two of you fill me in?"

"Boss, you change girls more than I change underwear, and you've always said that you never told a single one what you did and that none would ever find out. Then this girl shows up, already knowing who we were, what we did, and how to find us. Does that not scream surveillance?" John questioned, keeping his voice down.

"It's just a little strange to us," Tony added.

Just as Tony finished his sentence, I heard a thud coming from my bedroom that sounded like a phone had been dropped. I held my hand up to the guys and looked back at the hallway. Once I saw the A/C vent, it clicked in my head. Sound traveled annoyingly well through the vents, and I could only assume she had heard us.

"Guys," I said as I pointed over my shoulder.

"Oh shit," John said in a whisper. "Now what?"

Chapter 33

Back in my bedroom, Veronica was panicking. She tried to control her breathing as she sent out a text message:

May have been compromised, roll out in unmarked units, secure perimeter, wait for my signal.

Once she regained control of her breathing, she gathered her overnight bag, took a look at herself in the mirror, and whispered to herself, *"You're okay. You are okay."*

When she finally opened the bedroom door, she was surprised to find us still in the kitchen sitting at the table. I made eye contact with her and just smiled.

"There she is," John said, helping himself to another piece of toast.

"Hey, good morning," Tony said as he moved to the couch and turned on the TV.

"Morning fellas, sorry I'm rushing out. Gotta open the bar today."

"What, no hug?" I said as I held out my arms.

"Oh, sorry," she hesitantly responded. As she moved toward me, she kept a close eye on where John and Tony were. She didn't know if we suspected her for sure yet, and she wasn't going to risk anything.

"Just a quick one, don't wanna keep the girls waiting."

Chapter 34

As soon as the words came out of her mouth, she knew her cover had just been blown. All three of us had just caught her in a lie. Tony sprang up from the couch, grabbing the spare gun he had hidden in between the cushions and the armrest and was now positioned between us and the door.

John walked to the counter and opened the random "junk drawer" that every kitchen had to grab his spare piece, just as Veronica pulled away.

"Just one question," I started as I held her hand. "Why would the girls be waiting if you're opening the bar?"

Veronica's eyes widened, and she ripped her hand out of mine, reached into her purse for a gun, and fired a blind shot at Tony as she dove behind the couch for cover. The shot barely missed his left shoulder, flying straight back into the wall. It was a surprisingly accurate shot considering her rapid movement.

Once she positioned herself firmly behind the couch, putting a TV tray between herself and the cushions for extra protection, she fired a few more shots at Tony, forcing him to circle back toward the kitchen, before firing multiple rounds at John and myself.

I had managed to flip the dining room table to the ground as bullets stuck into it. From my vantage point, I saw Tony trying to get a clean shot off. After a few less than good shots, we made eye contact, and I motioned him to get out through his bedroom window and get the car. Another shot was fired that broke through the table and struck the fridge, then silence.

I pointed John toward the stove that had taken a few rounds, and he crawled over to expose the gas line, then he crawled for the back door.

"So what's your name, sweetheart? We both know damn well it's not Veronica," I asked, trying to get a gauge on where she was.

"Tayler," she shouted back. "Put your gun down, Zack."

"No, I'm good. Who do you work for? I'd hate to kill the wrong person."

"You're not going to kill anyone. Put down your weapon and step out into the open."

"You first, honey," I said as John was waving me out. When I got to the door, he told me that he thought he'd seen undercover cops rolling down the street.

Chapter 35

Todd, that sneaky little bastard had finally gotten close enough that it was time to do something about it.

"Okay, I'm going to step out nice and slow," Tayler, or whatever her name was, said back in the house.

She stood up from behind the couch. Her gun was still pointed toward the kitchen with her shaky trigger finger waiting for my head to appear. She stood waiting until she heard the back screen door close behind me. When she realized I was already outside, she noticed the stove's new position, and that's when the stench of gas slapped her in the face. We made eye contact through the busted window, and I smiled as I pointed my gun to the exposed line.

"It's not you, honey, it's me," I said as I squeezed the trigger.

The bullet struck the back of the stove, causing a spark that ignited the gas, turning it into a massive ball of fire. Once it reached the gas main, it turned the stove into a missile. The explosion sent the stove flying through the house toward the front door. Tayler was barely able to get the door shut, giving her some protection, but it still wasn't enough.

The three of us were cutting through the neighborhood, zig-zagging our way back toward the main roads, and ditching the car at the nearest intersection, where we continued on foot through a parking lot. We came rushing out of some shrubs that lined the street, just barely avoiding a student driver that, no doubt, wasn't prepared for that scare.

I ran around to the driver's side door, swung it opened, and said, "Don't worry, sweetheart, you passed."

On the other side, John wasn't near as gentle, pulling the instructor out by his tie and screaming for him to back up to the curb.

"Are you fucking kidding me?" Tony shouted.

"That was too fucking close. What the hell do we do now? Undercovers will be on our ass in minutes, our house is in flames, and we have nobody to trust, let alone that trusts us," John added.

"Do either of you have a phone? Mine's probably melted," I asked, staying as calm as possible.

"Who the hell are you calling?" Tony asked as he tossed up his phone.

Chapter 36

"I swear this city never sleeps."

"Yeah, the phones have been ringing all morning. What's going on?"

"From what I gather, there's a shots fired call. Here's your coffee, sir."

Officer Jones wasn't anything more than a paper pusher for the department; the closest he ever gets to walk the streets was getting his boss' morning coffee and sprinkles. However, Jones was in charge of knowing everything about every single undercover operation in the city, making him irreplaceable in Todd's eyes.

"You know it's going to be a bad day when people are shooting at each other before breakfast," Todd said as his phone began to ring. "Todd."

"I never thought I'd see the day that the captain would send a female in to do his dirty work."

"Brown?" Todd asked as he motioned for Jones to start a trace.

"No, it's the fucking Easter Bunny. I knew you were desperate to catch me but sending someone else to take your fall? Now that's low."

As Todd looked up to see how far Jones had made it on the trace, he couldn't help but notice the panicked look on his face.

"Where are you, Brown?" Todd asked as Jones came rushing into his office.

"Sir, we received a message this morning from one of our alias' phones, more specifically Tayler's, saying their mission had been compromised!"

"Little busy here," Todd interrupted.

"Sir, we tracked the number. It was at the same address as the shots fired calls we've been getting. And we just got another call reporting an explosion."

"An explosion?" Todd questioned, his heart seeming to stop.

"Yeah, you know how sensitive an exposed gas line can be. All it takes is a little spark." As soon as I finished talking, I tossed the phone out of the window.

"Sir, we lost the trace."

"Get Ryan and Stevens on the phone and have them meet me at that address now," Todd said as he rushed out of his office.

Chapter 37

Todd was racing through the precinct, shouting for everyone he passed to gear up and follow him to the scene. Once he had reached his car, he began to coordinate with the NYFD and paramedics. All the while, he had one thought circling through his mind. *He* had been the cause of an officer's death. Sure, he didn't pull the trigger, but who gave the order? Who sent her undercover?

He was going to have to live with that, being reminded every day when he'd have to walk past the "Fallen Heroes" wall outside his office. The more the guilt grew, so did the anger.

"I knew he was a good for nothing shit bag, but all the years I've known him, been chasing him—hell all the time I've spent studying him—I never thought he'd kill an officer in cold blood."

"Captain Todd, come in," a voice crackled over the radio.

"Go for Todd."

"Sir, it's Ryan—"

"What's the situation?" Todd shouted into the radio, cutting off his detective.

"I just pulled up. The house is in flames, debris everywhere. I've gotten as far as trying to keep spectators back and making a path for paramedics."

"Are there any survivors?"

"Brown isn't here if that's what you're asking."

"I'm aware of that."

"Then why ask about survivors?"

There was a long pause as Todd was contemplating his answer. The whole situation was spinning out of control. He trusted a known dirty cop, who could still be lying to him. He put a rookie undercover to get close to one of the most dangerous thugs in the city, and he'd kept his best detective in the dark.

"Because I had a UC there," he finally said.

"An undercover? Who?" Ryan questioned.

"Tayler."

"You put a rookie undercover without telling me? I'm supposed to be the primary on this investigation."

"The decision was made above your head, detective. Now find her, I'll be there in five," Todd said, tossing his radio to the side and pushing down the accelerator of his unmarked '02 Impala.

Chapter 38

"Stevens, get over here."

"What the hell happened?" Stevens said, looking around in shock.

"Brown, that's what happened."

"What do you mean?"

"Brown is a wild animal, and when you corner a wild animal, it fucking attacks," Ryan shouted, taking his frustrations out on the junior detective.

"So Brown blew up his own house? What would make him do that?"

"Our obsessed captain sent in an undercover office, a rookie, and she was found out," Ryan explained.

"Todd sent in a UC? He should've told you, at least, you're the primary."

"I don't know. Something tells me that there is quite a bit the good captain hasn't told us."

"What should we do?"

"Right now, I want you to set up a perimeter, 50 yards in every direction. Nobody gets in or out unless it's Todd, paramedics, or I say so," Ryan said as he ran his hands through his hair and gazed back at what was left of the house.

The fire department had already doused the flames, and all that remained was charred support beams. To his right, Ryan saw a busted TV and what appeared to be the rest of the living room furniture. He turned to his left to see firefighters spraying water on a few hot spots and moving anything that was charred to the street to prevent flare-ups.

In front of him, just outside the door frame, he saw the kitchen stove lying on the front door. He assumed it's where the hose jockeys must have dropped it until he noticed a slight shift coming from under the door.

Ryan scrambled to the door and lifted it as if it were a feather pillow to reveal Tayler, barely conscious.

"I need a medic!" Ryan shouted back as he rolled her onto her back.

"Stand back," a medic said as he rushed up.

"Stay with me with me, baby," Ryan said as he fell back to a knee.

Chapter 39

"We've got a pulse," one medic said as he strapped an oxygen mask around her ears.

"We need to get her loaded up; we can't help her here," another one said.

Ryan was frozen in both shock and disbelief. The sight of Tayler barely moving, with shrapnel in all of her limbs, and blood running down her face from a three-inch cut that ran across her forehead was almost too much for him. Her once white, now crimson shirt had been cut off so heart rate monitors could be attached, was tossed at his feet as they secured her to a stretcher.

Still in shock, Ryan followed them down the walkway, gripping her hand until they reached the back of the ambulance, and he was forced to let it go. He watched the ambulance until it rounded the corner and sped out of sight.

"Ryan, Todd just pulled up," Stevens called out, but the lead detective didn't respond.

"Hey, Ryan, you with me, man?" Stevens tried again, this time grabbing his shoulder, which jerked him out of his trance.

"What?" Ryan said.

"Todd's here. He wants to be brought up to speed."

The sight of him climbing out of his car immediately enraged Ryan. His hands began to shake as he headed toward him with Stevens on his heels.

"You son of a bitch!" he shouted as they got close enough to where nobody else could hear.

"Excuse me?"

"You had no right to send in my wife without my knowledge!" Ryan continued.

"Ex-wife," Todd replied. "And I don't have to tell you anything I don't want to. Perks of being the captain."

"You stupid, obsessed, bastard!" Ryan continued shouting as Stevens made his way in between them.

"You should've at least told us you sent in an undercover."

"Jerry, we're chasing a downright psychopath. God only knows how many people he's killed. I didn't tell anyone because I thought he had people in my office. Turns out, I was right about that," Todd said, walking away from his upset officers. "Now, we need to find out where he's going. That's where you come in."

Ryan sped up to pass his partner and stood face to face with Todd. "Either you tell me why you're so obsessed with Brown, or you take my badge and find him yourself."

Chapter 40

The sun had just started to set, and we were still driving through the city. We had another place we could hide out, but if Todd had gotten an undercover cop to sleep with me for information, I didn't want to risk him having a team waiting on us.

There hadn't been a word spoken between the three of us in a couple of hours. I could feel both of them looking at me, wondering how I, of all people, could've let something like this happen.

Maybe I'd been slacking, gotten soft. Could it be? Perhaps I'd become so complacent with the "ghost" reputation that I dropped my guard. Did I owe the guys an explanation? I had nearly gotten them arrested, right?

I made a sharp, quick turn into a parking garage, cutting off an Arab who blasted the horn of his taxi and sped up the ramp of a parking garage until I found a spot on the fourth floor. I stopped short and slammed the car in park, then killed the engine.

"What now?" John asked.

"We could go uptown, to the loft?" Tony suggested.

"I'm sorry, guys," I said, not looking away from the city lights that sparkled in front of me.

"What?"

"I'm sorry," I repeated.

"What the fuck for?" Tony asked.

"You just saved our asses."

"Yeah, after I put you in that spot."

"Boss, seriously, there's no way you could've known she was NYPD. None of us had ever seen her," John said, trying to make me feel better.

"You guys sniffed it out."

"Well, we weren't sleeping with her either."

"And then you also made her pay for it."

"We aren't mad at you, Zack. We've been in tight spots before and come out just fine," Tony said as he jabbed me in the arm.

"True story," John said. "It was kinda cool that you blew up a house with a stove and a bullet. You were acting like *MacGyver*?"

"Yeah, no shit, Mr. Unpredictable is back."

And that's when it hit me. I suddenly knew how to get this job done—be unpredictable.

Chapter 41

"Come on, boys, we've gotta move," I said, climbing out of the car. It was safe to assume that the driving instructor had reported the car stolen by now. Especially since half of New York's police department were all over the neighborhood.

The three of us headed to the staircase that ran up and down the middle of the garage and hurried to the second floor. Once the police found the driver's ed car, they'd start looking for another missing vehicle, and at least stealing one from a different floor would slow them down, hopefully.

We found a dark blue '04 Mustang, with up-to-date inspection, registration, and tinted windows. There was nothing really special about it, which is exactly why we chose it. As we moved closer, I scanned the entire floor. It was empty, nobody walking to their car, nobody looking for a spot, and just like the stairs, no cameras.

John backed up to the driver's window, looked around once more, and smashed the window with his elbow. Naturally, the alarm started blaring. Tony jumped in and frantically began to hotwire it. Within two minutes, the alarm stopped, and the engine fired up. John got into the passenger seat, and I climbed into the back. Tony drove us out of the garage and headed west on 42nd street. In my daze, I hadn't realized where I drove when we left the house. We'd gone from Brooklyn to damn near Central Park.

"We're going to Seri's loft," I said as I laid down in the back seat.

"Why of all places would we go to Seri's?"

"He wants an update, I'm sure. Plus, we're without lodging at the moment."

"He's gonna flip shit if we show up there," John said.

"And there's no way he's gonna let us stay there."

"Well, we're not going to. We're going to swing by and let him know what's going on, leave the car there, and then head to the safe house. And tomorrow, we take out Natano."

"Zack, we're not ready for that," John said, turning to look at me.

"We've got nothing planned, how are we going to do that?" Tony asked.

"All in due time."

Chapter 42

"Hey Malorie, I'd like to introduce you to Detectives Ryan and Stevens, two of my best," Captain Todd said as he held open the front door of his home.

"Oh, well, hello boys," Mrs. Todd said as she dried her hands off on the towel that hung from her apron. "Are you boys staying for dinner? We've got plenty."

"Gentleman, this is my beautiful wife, Malorie," Todd said as he kissed her on the cheek.

"Mrs. Todd, it's an absolute pleasure to finally meet you," Ryan said.

"The captain's office is full of pictures of you two and your children," Stevens added.

"Oh, please call me Mal. That's how everyone knows me."

"Where are the kiddos, speaking of? I'd love to meet them."

"Well, Mark is actually staying at his friend's house, and Maryanne is upstairs. She'll be down for dinner," Mal replied.

"Honey, we're actually going to go to my study to compare notes about a case. Would you mind if we skipped out on dinner?"

"I'm not going to let the three of you go without eating; you boys will just have to take a plate with you," Mal said as she waved a finger at Todd's nose.

Ryan and Stevens thanked Mrs. Todd and made a plate of roasted chicken, green beans, and mashed potatoes, all made from scratch, before following their boss into the far back room his wife let him turn into a study.

"You have a beautiful family, sir," Stevens said as he shut the door.

"Thank you, Jerry," Todd said as he took a bite of his wife's excellent cooking.

"With all due respect, sir, I'm not here for roasted chicken. You owe us an explanation," Ryan said.

"Make no mistake about it, Ryan, I don't owe you a goddamn thing," Todd said just before there was a knock at the door.

"Daddy?" a voice said on the other side.

"Come on in, baby. Guys, this is my daughter."

The two detectives said their hellos and sat in silence as Todd asked his youngest how school was and listened to every detail about the boy who had a crush on her and how much she hated math. Say what you will about Greg Todd, the man was a fantastic husband and father. Once Maryanne finished describing her day, her father told her to be sure the door shut behind her and gave her a kiss goodnight.

"All right, boys, pay attention. This will be the last time you hear this."

Chapter 43

"Before Mark and Maryanne, before Malorie, before I joined the force, I didn't always make the best decisions," Todd said as he poured three glasses of brandy, the perfect after-dinner drink.

"Sir, we were all young once. We all did stupid things," Stevens said.

"That may be true, but listen to the rest of the story."

Before Todd continued, he took a sip of his brandy, reached into the bottom drawer, and, with a key, took out the false bottom.

"You two are the only people I've ever shown this to," he said as he placed an old picture on the desk.

"What the hell?"

"Captain, is that...?"

"Yeah, that's Brown with his arm around my shoulders."

Stevens couldn't believe it. Here he'd felt so guilty for so long about helping Brown get away with so much, and he was on Todd's buddy list?

"We grew up in the same building, played at the same park—we were friends. That picture was taken over 20 years ago," Todd began to explain.

"*Were* friends?" Ryan asked. "With all due respect, people usually don't hang on to photos of people they *used* to be friends with."

"Ryan, you're from Upper Manhattan, right?"

"Yeah, so?"

"Well, in my experience, people from your neighborhood have live-in nannies, private schools, that kinda stuff, right?"

"Still looking for your point."

"When you grow up with nothing, you hold your friends close. They become family. There was a time I would've done anything for him."

"Then what happened?" Stevens asked.

"In our neighborhood, the mob basically ran everything. I saw men shot over gambling debts and beaten until they were unrecognizable because they looked at the wrong person. It was a life I swore my children would never see."

"Is that why you joined the force?"

"There was a bar fight one night, and the five of us happened to be walking by; naturally, the mob was involved. It spilled out into the street, and I'm not sure how, but we got in the middle of it. We had different ideas—I wanted to hang back, but Zack wanted to jump in."

"Well, from everything we know about him, that's not surprising," Ryan said.

"Of course, Tony, John, and Brian followed his every move. I went across the street and could see the four of them taking on four or five at a time, but I wasn't the only one who noticed," Todd said as his face filled with remorse, like what happened next was his fault.

Chapter 44

Todd took a minute to compose himself and to pour another round of drinks. He leaned back in his chair and cracked a half-smile and rubbed his forehead.

"Shots rang out, and I could see at least three guys hit the ground. I ducked behind a bench for cover and to avoid being seen, but when I heard Zack ask if everyone was good, I peeked back up. I saw Senior, Sokolov's father, walk up to the guys, shake their hands, and express his gratitude for their help."

"As a teenager, he impressed Sokolov?" Ryan asked. "I don't know which one that says more about."

"Zack was pissed that I didn't jump into the fight. We argued about it for days, until one day he came to my apartment and told me that I could either come with them to their new job or forget we were ever friends."

"The new job with the family?" Stevens asked.

"I thought about it, I really did. But after all we'd seen and been through as kids, I just knew I had to do something to at least try and make this city better for my children," Todd explained.

"He took his 'best friends' into the mob? That sounds like he never cared."

"You got it backward, Ryan. That's exactly why he took them, to keep an eye on them."

"Then why didn't you go?" Stevens asked.

"I just couldn't. Call it whatever you will, but I think it was fate. That's why I forgot about it. I moved on, focused on school, graduated, and joined the force," Todd said as he took another sip.

"So why the obsession?" Ryan asked.

"About seven years ago, I got into a little trouble, made a mistake, and got bummed to traffic for a few weeks as punishment. I made a routine stop, some college chick speeding, and I was in the cruiser writing the ticket when three guys came rushing out of an alley and rushed the car."

"Brown and the guys?" Ryan asked.

"She freaked and got out of the car, screaming. I got out of my car, identified myself, and all three of them stopped. The driver motioned, and the other two got in the car like I wasn't even there."

"He knew it was you based on your voice?"

"Brown turned around, smiled, and without hesitating, he shot a single round into my left shoulder, through and through. He obviously had forgotten our past, just like he said he would."

"He just turned and shot you? That's cold-blooded," Ryan said.

"I got promoted soon after that and began focusing on organized crime, mainly for revenge on Brown. The more cases I worked or reviewed, the more I realized how dangerous he is. I want him off my streets."

"Why didn't you tell us this before?" Stevens asked.

"I don't want anyone knowing about my past; I'm doing everything I can to protect my family."

Chapter 45

Seri was sitting in his usual booth, the last one in the back left corner behind the pool tables, with his beloved and nephew sitting across from him. He was drinking double vodkas, two at a time, looking over the ledgers of his businesses, making sure both his legitimate money and off the book cash added up.

"Two more, please," he shouted toward the bar.

The bartender rolled her eyes, made the two drinks, and handed them to Joey, who took them to his uncle.

"So, how's the Natano case coming along?" Joey asked.

"They've got six days to deliver," Seri said after downing one of his drinks.

"And if they don't?"

"Then, I will take care of them."

"Easier said than done, I'm assuming," Joey said.

"Seri, it's late, time to go home," Natalya said from across the table.

"Controlling bitch," Seri said under his breath as he gathered all his papers.

"Hey, Joe, why don't you come by the house tomorrow? We'll watch the game."

"Yeah, sounds good."

It took about ten minutes to get from the bar to their loft. The whole time, Natalya had her face buried in a magazine, which annoyed Seri. He liked being the center of her attention.

When the two of them got home, Natalya went to take a shower, and before Seri could pour another drink, the doorbell rang. Seri grabbed his gun, just as a precaution, swung the door open, and was shocked to see Tony and John standing there.

"What the hell are you two doing here?" he asked.

"What's the matter, Seri? We can't just drop by?" Tony said as he pushed his way into the loft.

"How'd you even know about this place?" Seri asked as he walked into the living room and turned on the lights.

"Because we are that damn good," I said as the lights lit up the room. The sight of me sitting on his couch made Seri's jaw drop. That was the first time in years I'd seen him surprised.

"We need to talk."

Chapter 46

"Talk? What the hell do we need to talk about?" Seri asked.

"The weather, what do you think?" I said sarcastically.

"What's there to talk about? You have six days to finish your job, and if you don't, I take care of you, plain and simple."

"Not that simple, give us some credit," John said.

"What do you guys want?"

"We wanted to tell you; we're making our move on Natano tomorrow," Tony said.

"Tomorrow? Why tomorrow?" Seri questioned.

"Why not?" I asked.

"So, you guys have a plan?" Seri asked. He wasn't thrilled about this because his "spy" hadn't told him about any plan.

"We know he goes to the same bar at least twice a week. If he's there, we eliminate any bodyguards first, grab him, and put a bullet in his head."

"*If* he's there?" Seri asked. "You've been at this for a week, and you don't even know if he'll be there?"

"We hit a little speed bump," I said.

"What the hell do you mean, speed bump?"

"Our intel may have been compromised. Long story short, we're going to make it up as we go."

"Make it up? What the fuck do you mean?" Seri shouted.

"What's wrong with that?" Tony asked.

"Where do I start? Do you know how many things could go wrong? What if he has multiple people with him? What if you mess up and leave a witness?"

"Seri, how long have you known us? We don't mess up, and we can handle anything that's thrown at us," I said. "Besides, I'm sure you know a little about his life, am I right?"

"What's that supposed to mean?" Seri asked.

"It means you can tell us what he's up to probably better than anyone else. You can tell us when he's most likely to have his guard down, the best time for us to make our move."

Chapter 47

"I'm going to tell you?" Seri asked.

"Yes, sir, the way I see it, who would know Natano's life better than you?" I replied.

"Why the fuck would I help you?" Seri asked. "You work for me, not the other way around."

"Boys, give us a couple of minutes. Go see if Natalya is as hot naked as she is covered," I said as the boys started moving to the other room.

"If you touch her, I'll chop your balls off," Seri said, pointing at them.

"We'll be in here," John said as they walked into the living room.

Seri was steaming. He was pacing back and forth as I continued to sit on his couch.

"You got balls, Brown. I'll give you that. You break into my house and expect me to help."

"Look, this can happen one of two ways—you can tell me what you know, like the best time to move on him, and the job gets done nice and easy. Or I can wing it, and it could get messy. The choice is yours."

"What makes you think I would even know that much about him?"

"Same reason I know where you live—you keep tabs on the people you want dead," I said, looking straight into his eyes.

Seri thought about what he was going to say next. Helping us help him made sense to a point, but he wasn't about to agree without considering every aspect of the situation.

"Natano has a diner he usually goes to for lunch, 54th and Grand. It's a safe bet that he'll be there tomorrow," Seri said.

"54th and Grand? I know the area."

"Tomorrow around one, then?" Seri said. "Just think, in about 24 hours, you'll be out."

Chapter 48

I got the guys, and we left Seri's loft. When we got out of the building, we hailed a cab to take us to an apartment building in Queens. As usual, we were silent the whole ride. The cab pulled up to a building that wasn't upscale, but it wasn't a total dump; I mean, it still probably had more roaches than residents, but hell, this in New York. We got out of the cab, paid, and made our way to the back of the building.

Tony knelt down and picked the lock to a door that led to a stairwell. It's not that we were sneaking in; we're just a little camera shy, and it's easier to hide your face in a stairwell than in a lobby. The door opened, and we went up to the second floor, where John led us to the room we kept reserved for emergencies. It was basically empty except for what was built in. The only things in the room were a table with chairs, a bed, and two sofa beds, but looks can be deceiving.

I walked to the bed, flipped the mattress, and in the hollowed-out box spring, was a sawed-off shotgun, three .9mm handguns, three military-grade combat knives, and my personal favorite, a Colt .45. I picked up my gun and, out of habit, went to the table and started cleaning it.

"Why are we here?" Tony asked as he pulled out the small arsenal, he stored inside the wall behind the drop-down ironing board.

"Yeah, I didn't think we'd be here of all places," John said, to nobody's surprise, heading straight for the alcohol.

"Well, I'm glad I can still keep you two guessing," I said.

"Seriously, man, what's going on?"

"Tomorrow afternoon, we finish the Natano job," I started. "And if I'm going to do something I told Senior I wouldn't, I might as well use the piece he left me."

"Zack, you can't feel guilty about this," John said.

"The fuck I can't. Senior was basically a father to me, hell to all three of us. And because his son is a little bitch, we're about to do the one thing we promised we wouldn't do."

"You don't think we're feeling the same thing?" John asked. "There's nothing we can do about it now. Senior would understand."

"I know he would, but it's the fact that Seri gave the fucking order," I said, still cleaning the Colt. "Bottom line, we get out tomorrow. Let's focus on that."

John grinned, slapped my back, and headed to the kitchen to grab beer for the three of us.

"This will make you feel better."

"If I start drinking, I'll shut up."

"That's the plan," Tony said with a smile.

Chapter 49

The three of us were up before the sun. Honestly, I don't think any of us fully went to sleep. We were a mixture of nervous, excited, scared, and maybe five or six other emotions. This was the only life we'd ever really known, and in roughly ten hours, it'd be over. Then what? Apply at Chase Manhattan?

"Should we get breakfast?" Tony asked.

"So you can throw up in an alley? No, we'll pass," I said.

"Not even coffee?"

"No," I said, annoyed. "You guys know the drill. This is not the time to start changing the routine."

"We already are," John said. "We gotta stop to pick up Joey. Might as well get some damn eggs."

"No, dammit."

"Loosen up, boss, we're just talking out loud to ease the tension."

"It's very annoying."

"Everything is to you. It's game day, and you're just anxious."

They weren't wrong; every job was the same. On the day of, I would be annoyed by every single little thing. There was always so much planning involved, so every detail had to be perfect. I was a little surprised myself that I was so irritable since we didn't have a plan. It wasn't until I turned on to the street that Joey's apartment was on that it hit me. It was the fact that we had to take this dumbass with us.

Chapter 50

"I can see them. They're in an old Ford, just turned on the street."

"We can see them."

"I'm nervous. What if they find out I called you?"

"Well, if you don't mention it, I doubt they'll figure it out."

"Seriously? You have met these guys, right?"

"Just stay calm, and stick to the plan."

"Do you know how many plans I have to stick to right now? And no disrespect, but your last plan wasn't exactly great."

"That's why this one is so great. They'd never expect it, coming from you."

"I'm not sure about this."

"Well, it's a little late to back out. Just think what would happen to you if you did."

"Is that a threat?"

"No, see, I'm not stupid enough to bite the hand that feeds me."

"I can still call this off."

"Actually, since we can see you and the car, you really have no choice. Just stick to the plan, and everyone walks away."

"Including my uncle?"

"Joe, as long as he cooperates, there will be no problem. Just be sure he does."

"Okay fine. I can do this, but it's not for you. Just stay close."

"We'll be right behind you. Just act normal."

Chapter 51

"Well, look at this, he's actually waiting on us."

"Probably worried we'd leave his ass here."

I pulled up next to him, blocked a fire hydrant, put the car in park, and the three of us got out of the car. I leaned against the driver's door while John and Tony walked around the car so we could all three be face to face with Joey.

"What's going on? Are we doing this or what?"

"Calm down, Joe. Just need to go over a few things," Tony said.

"I don't think I should know any more than I already do. Plausible deniability, ya know?"

"Who the fuck said we were going to tell you anything?" John said as he smacked the back of his head.

"Then what do I need to hear?"

"Look, Joey, you're a good kid. Completely ignorant of how your uncle is using you, but a good kid."

"Get to the point, Zack."

"We have a job to do, and to us, this is a very important one."

"Yeah, I know that, Ser: has already brought me up to speed."

"That's why it's important to him, not to us. Bottom line, stay out of the way, or you will not be coming home tonight."

"Don't worry, I'm just driving, right? That's what I do best."

"For your sake, I hope so. Follow every traffic law, use your blinker, don't speed, and if you see a car stay with us for more than two turns, change course, understood?"

"Yes, sir."

"All right, what are we waiting for? Let's get to it."

Chapter 52

Paul Natano stood at six feet, eight inches tall, and weighed a solid 260, all muscle. His only vice was Maggie's, a hole in the wall diner that apparently had the best grilled cheeses in the state. Seri's intel had paid off. He was there just like he said he would be.

We could see him in a booth, second from the wall, with two other people I didn't recognize.

"How do you wanna do this?" John asked.

"As smooth as possible," I replied.

"It's 11:30 on a Saturday morning. How could this possibly go smooth?" Joey asked.

"You leave that to us," Tony said.

"John, do a walk by, get a headcount, then cut down the alley between the buildings, to the back door; shoot Tony a text when you get there."

"You got it," John said as he climbed out of the car.

"Won't Natano recognize him?" Joey asked. I sighed and looked at him, hoping to shut him up.

"Okay, I'll be quiet."

For the next few minutes, we sat there just watching John cross the street and make his way past the diner. As he got closer, he propped up his collar and put on sunglasses. Once he got in front of the diner, he bent down as if to tie his shoe, peered into the door, then rushed toward the alley. About 45 seconds later, Tony's phone buzzed.

3 at Natano's table, 2 at table in back, 1 cook, 1 server. Picking lock. Heading to kitchen.

"Tony, get in there and convince the other table that it'd be in their best interest to leave, now."

"What do you want me to do?" Joey asked as Tony shut his door and jogged across the street, entered the diner, and pulled up a chair to the couple enjoying their lunch.

"Head up around the corner—the first low profile car you find, take it, go two blocks east; we'll meet you in the middle of the street. Hurry up," I said as I handed him a *Slim Jim*.

"We're changing cars?"

"Did I tell you to take it?" I said, staring a hole into him. "Move your ass— you've got ten minutes."

Chapter 53

"Hey Pauly, how ya been?"

"Ya know, just once, I'd love to enjoy a nice lunch, without a fucking slimeball like you coming around asking for a handout."

"Pauly, we go back. We've been friends since we were kids."

"No, Danny, that's where you're wrong, you've been mooching off my family since we were kids."

"Pauly, please, I need your help."

"What is it this time, gambling? Spend more than you have at the track?"

"Why do you hate me so much? What could I have possibly done?"

The truth of the matter is, Danny really didn't do anything to Paul. He just tried to take care of his family. Unfortunately, that meant Paul's number two man was sentenced to six years in Bayview Correctional Facility.

Paul took that personally. Danny had been around for years, and he knew just about everything there was to know about Natano's operation. Depending on who you asked, Paul would rather have been locked up than anyone in his circle. It seems honorable enough, but it was actually a selfish motive. He knew he'd never say anything about his own operation, but other people can be bought or scared into saying just about anything.

Not Paul, though. His physical appearance alone was enough to make normal people avoid eye contact. Any ex-con in New York would tell you that the guards in Bayview got off on the punishment that they could inflict on former gangsters. Natano's men were loyal, but every man hits a point where they just can't take it anymore.

"My friend is doing time because of you. Why would I even listen to you?" Paul said.

"I was looking out for my family. I thought in your business that's something that was to be respected."

"Maybe in the old days; nowadays, you cross the boss, you get cut off."

"I've been your friend for years, and you won't even hear me out?"

Paul looked at Danny, thought about everything they had been through as friends, and decided not to overreact.

"Sit down," he finally said.

"Thank you, Pauly. Who's he?"

"This is the man I let follow me around with a loaded gun. In other words, don't fucking worry about it."

"Always were paranoid."

"Hold on a second, who's that?"

"You're probably just seeing things," Danny said without looking.

"No, no, no, I'm sure I've seen him before."

Chapter 54

I walked across the street, thinking that this couldn't be real; it didn't feel real. I leaned against a mailbox and pretended to check my phone. I glanced up and saw that John had made his way into the kitchen and was forcing the cook out with his gun pointed at the back of his head. I turned and saw that Tony had pulled his gun and put it on the table of the only other couple inside. The couple shared a look of panic and hurried out the door, leaving their coats hanging on the backs of their chairs.

"Great seeing you guys, I'll let you know about the Hamptons," I heard Tony shout as they rushed past me. I couldn't help but smile. Tony had a gift of manipulation that was just fun to watch.

I opened the door, gave Tony a hug like I haven't seen him in years, and the two of us sat ourselves in the booth behind the table Natano was conducting his business.

"It's been too long, how are you? How's that beauty queen you're married to?"

"Just fine, spending more in a week than I make in a month," I said as we shared a fake laugh.

I sat with my back toward Natano so that I was directly behind his muscle. I took off my jacket and reached deep into my chest pocket for my .45, crossed my arms, and leaned back in my seat with the barrel of the gun pointed into the vinyl seat.

"Tell me, how are the boys?" I asked, carrying on our charade.

"They're growing like weeds."

"Excuse me; we're in the middle of business here. Move your asses to the other side of the diner, now," Natano's muscle said, trying to strike fear into us.

"Oh no, excuse us, we're in the middle of something very important," I said without turning my head. My eyes were locked on Tony, waiting for him to nod, telling me when to move.

"Take care of these fucking idiots," Natano said to his muscle.

Tony shook his head right as the nameless man started to make his move. I took a deep breath, and when I exhaled, I fired two shots through the booth into his back. The first one entered just below his ribs and punctured his liver. The second lodged into his spine, instantly paralyzing him.

Danny got up to flee the scene and ran straight into Tony, who spun him around and was able to get him into a headlock with his gun pressed to his temple.

I stood up from the table and turned, gun drawn, to see Natano already standing with one gun pointed at me and one at Tony.

"You two really screwed up."

"Depends on which side you're on."

"I could easily kill your friend here," Tony said.

"Go ahead, save me the trouble."

"Drop the guns, Paul," I said as I took a step toward him.

"A lot bigger fish have tried to take me down. What makes you two think you have a chance?"

"I guess you're right," I said as I tucked my gun into my waistline. "I'm just curious why you only think there are two of us."

The wheels in Paul's head started to spin. He kept looking back and forth at me and Tony. After a minute or two, Paul lost his patience. He dropped the gun that was pointed at Tony and took a step toward me.

"Say goodbye," he said as he put the gun to my forehead.

Just as he was ready to pull the trigger, John whistled. Paul jerked his head around to see who got the drop on him, only to catch a frying pan to the left cheek.

Chapter 55

"What the hell took you so long?"

"The cook wanted to be Mr. Getbad there for a minute," John said as he tossed the frying pan on the table.

"He could've shot you, boss."

"Good thing I had backup then."

"What do we do about this one?" John asked, pointing to Paul's friend, Danny.

"Tie them up, back to back, in those chairs," I said after I thought about that for a minute. "Guys, still want coffee?"

"Yeah, why not?" John replied with a smile.

"I take mine with two sugars," Danny said.

"Oh, gosh," I started. "You see, we would, but you won't be around long enough to enjoy it."

That statement made Danny start groveling, begging to be set free, promising that he'd never tell anyone what he saw.

"Shut him up," I said.

I grabbed three mugs and filled them for the guys and me. I watched John drag Natano's limp body and lift him into a chair. Tony had already finished restraining Danny and was stuffing his own socks into his mouth.

"Now what?" he asked.

"Now, let's have our coffee, then we'll make this look sloppy, I mean really sloppy," I said.

This wasn't like us; we were basically waiting for someone to walk in and see us, which is what we wanted. We had always been ghosts, never left a witness, and now, we were begging someone to come in and catch us. It took about three minutes for someone to walk in.

She couldn't have been more than 23. She had very curly red hair and was wearing a green sweater, khaki pants, and carrying a laptop. She had her headphones in, and when she saw Natano and Danny, bound and gagged, her expression turned to panic.

"What the hell is going on?" she asked, pulling out her headphones.

"Oh, honey, as much fun as you would be, I'm going to have to ask you to keep moving," Tony said, walking toward her with his gun at his side.

As she backed out of the door, she began crying for help—that's when I started waking up Natano

"Rise and shine, sweetheart."

"What do you want?" he asked, barely moving his head.

"I just want you to know who killed you. I'm actually surprised you let us get so close."

"I…I don't…understand," he said, still barely awake.

"It's us—John, Tony, and me, Zack."

"Sokolov."

"That's right, Pauly. Say hi to your father," I said as I pulled the trigger.

The bullet entered his head slightly off-center, above the right eye. His head fell forward, and blood started pouring from his wound to the floor.

Danny was screaming through his gag so hard that he was almost choking. I was so lost in my own world that I barely heard him. I was just staring at Natano's lifeless body. This isn't my first, far from it, so I don't know if it was the usual feeling of completing a job or the fact that it was Natano's body I was looking at that was so mesmerizing. The sound of John's gun firing into Danny's temple finally jolted me back to reality.

I looked up, and Tony was at the front, locking the door and flipping the sign from "open" to "closed," and John was whipping our prints off of the armrests and his gun.

"Wait a second, John, is that a burner?"

"Yeah, no cereal number. Not my first time."

"I got an idea—untie Danny, and put the gun in his hand."

"Murder-suicide, I like it," Tony said.

"Hurry up, let's bail out the back," I said as we walked through the kitchen and storage space, out the back door, then started heading east.

Chapter 56

"Where the hell did you go? The car is empty."

"Brown made me ditch the car and get a new one."

"We can see the diner, looks like there are two people inside sitting back to back."

"Only two? There were at least five that I could see."

"Shit, they've already offed them. Get hold of forensics; get them here ASAP," Todd said to Jones. "While you're at it, get Stevens, Ryan, and Tayler down here."

"Todd, I'm supposed to pick them up two blocks east of the diner."

"Okay, Joey, keep to the plan, we'll figure out what happened here. Keep your GPS on, and we'll track your location."

"All right, hurry up, though. I'm supposed to be taking them to the river to meet my uncle."

Todd hung up his cell, got out of his unmarked car, and sprinted across the street while Jones tried to keep spectators at bay. He reached for the doorknob and turned it back and forth. After a few seconds, he squared up and kicked the door in.

He checked the pulse of both Natano and Danny. Once he felt nothing, he swept his eyes from the back wall to the front on the left side of the restaurant, looking under the tables just to be sure. After that side was clear, he moved on to the booths.

The first one was empty, the second was clear as well, the third had a hole in the backrest, and the fourth, he found a white male, two gunshots in the back, DOA.

Todd cleared him of his weapon, double-checked the last booth, and rushed toward the kitchen. Empty. All he found was an open door leading to a loading dock.

As he walked back to the dining room, Todd holstered his weapon and started running the scenario through his head. He knew there was more than met the eye here. He heard the sirens in the distance, so he took a minute, leaned against the wall, and waited for his team to arrive.

Chapter 57

"You've got to think like him," Todd told himself as he scanned through the diner once more. "How would *he* have done this?"

Todd moved closer to the bodies for a better look. The one to his right had his hands tied behind his chair and severe swelling on the left side of his face. Probably a fractured jaw, maybe even orbital socket as well, indicating a struggle. His head was slumped forward so that his chin was resting on his chest, with blood and brain matter pooling at his feet, but there was no exit wound, suggesting a hollow point bullet may have been used. CSU would have to confirm that. He then turned his attention to the body on his left.

This John Doe had grabbed his interest. Unlike the other, this guy had no signs of struggle, indicating that he was running the show. There were no ligature marks, no swollen or bruised knuckles, nothing. But he was holding a gun. Tests would most likely confirm it was the same gun that fired the bullet into his temple.

Now on to the third, the man that was laid out in the back booth, what was his story? Todd leaned in to get a closer look, again taking note that there wasn't an exit wound for either bullet.

"Hell of a shot, or a bad break for you, bud," Todd said as he headed back to the front door.

Sirens were blaring, and cars were screeching to a stop as Todd stood at the door to ensure that nobody but Stevens, Ryan, and Tayler had the chance to fully go over the place before forensics took over the scene.

Chapter 58

"Huh, not what I was expecting," Tayler said as she walked in.

"Expecting a big ball of fire?" Ryan said.

"Funny. I just meant that it's cleaner than I pictured."

"He was calm, had control of this situation. When you were found out, his guard was down, he panicked. This is how good he is when he's focused," Todd explained.

"Let's not get ahead of ourselves," Ryan started. "At first glance, it looks like a murder-suicide, with a bystander who saw too much."

"No, there's more to this."

"That's why I said at first glance," Ryan shot back.

The tension between the captain and the head detective was still very high. Ryan had lost trust and respect for his boss. So how could he work with him? To make things worse, Todd didn't even seem to care.

"Stevens, recognize anyone?"

Stevens was still standing just inside the doorway, eyes locked on the two lifeless bodies that sat back to back.

"Stevens!" Tayler shouted.

"What?"

"Do you recognize anyone?"

"Yeah, the one on the right, that's Paul Natano."

"Natano?" Tayler said. "Wait, isn't that the guy Brown had you pull files on?"

"You tell me, you were sleeping with him," Stevens said.

"Fuck you."

"Stevens, you've been in bed with him a lot longer than she was," Ryan said.

"All of you, shut up," Todd intervened. "We're all in agreement that Brown is responsible for this, correct?"

"Yeah, no doubt about it."

"I'm not convinced," Ryan said. "Think about it—if everything you've told us, and if everything in his file is true, there would only be one body."

"How do you figure that?" Tayler asked.

"Not to bring up old shit, but look how they got to Stevens. They could've easily killed you that night," Ryan said.

"What's your point?"

"They're smart. Why would he leave a scene like this? Three bodies, one of which is still holding a gun."

"Are you really that green? Wow, and they call me a rookie," Stevens said.

"Excuse me?"

"It's staged, you moron."

"Staged?"

Chapter 59

Stevens and Ryan were squaring off. Ryan, out of spite, was trying to prove his partner, more importantly, his boss wrong. On the other side, Stevens was out to prove that he was just as good of a detective as Ryan.

"How did you get to that conclusion?" Tayler asked.

"About a week ago, Brown and his guys came and visited me at the station."

"There's no way. If he showed his face in my precinct, he'd either be in custody or dead," Todd said.

"Well, captain, sorry to disappoint you, but you've underestimated him."

"Again," Ryan added.

"Anyway, they cornered me and told me to get Natano's file. He said that in two weeks, they'd be out and gone."

"What do you mean gone?" Todd asked.

"Sokolov agreed to let them out after they finished this job."

"So, you're telling me that the three of them could already be in the wind?" Ryan asked.

"We can still get them—Brown, his guys, and Sokolov if we act fast," Todd said, not mentioning his contact with Joey.

"If we canvas the block, maybe we'll luck out and someone saw something," Tayler added.

"All right, Tayler, start looking around, let me know what you find," Todd started as his phone started to ring. "Hang on, you two."

"Todd, we don't have much time; we'd have a better shot at finding something if we all canvas," Ryan said.

"We caught a break. Brown was seen getting into a black sedan, two blocks east," Todd said.

"That doesn't make sense," Stevens said. "Who knows we're looking for him, and how did they know to call Todd?"

"I had contingency plans in place," Todd said over his shoulder.

"Oh, you've got to be kidding me," Ryan said. "What is this plan?"

"Never you mind."

Chapter 60

After we made our exit from the diner, we took our time heading for our driver, who was hopefully waiting on us. We walked down the sidewalk, making eye contact with people, smiling, wishing people a good day, and bragging about the Yankees. We made small talk with each other and other pedestrians that happened to be walking the same direction.

When we reached the end of the block, we waited for the light to change, and we crossed the street. We stopped on the corner and had a famous New York hotdog from a street cart before we headed down the next block to meet Joey.

I could see him on his phone in a dark sedan, halfway down the street, just like he was told. As we got closer to the car, I could see that Joey saw us, which caused him to act nervously as he hung up.

"You see that?" John asked.

"Relax, probably just Seri checking in," I said as I opened the passenger door and climbed in; Tony sat behind me, and John behind Joey.

"Is it done?"

"Would we be here if it wasn't?"

"Good point—I'll call my uncle, let him know we're on the way."

"Weren't you just on the phone with him?" John asked.

"That was my mother, actually. She calls me once a week."

"Isn't that sweet?" I said as Joey dialed. "Let's roll out."

"Seri is waiting for us at the docks. I know exactly where. We'll be there in ten minutes," Joey said as he pushed his phone back into his pocket.

Chapter 61

It was a quiet night in the city, the first time in a long time that I haven't heard sirens every few blocks. I would bet money that Todd had the whole city on alert. No doubt that he had every place that was ever associated with us under surveillance. I didn't even care; we were done. Todd could spin his wheels all he wanted. He would never find us.

"What are you guys going to do now?" Joey asked.

"Spearmint Rhino," Tony responded, causing everyone to chuckle a little.

"You would, bro," John said.

"You wouldn't?"

"Not at first. I have some cash saved up, might go back to the island, and visit."

"That's good, Johnny, it's been a while since you've gotten to go. What about you, boss?"

"Honestly, I have no idea. Probably just travel, see the world. Dust in the wind kinda thing," I replied.

"That's it?" Joey asked.

"Joe, when you make this your day job, the little things, like seeing the sights, seem that much better."

"That's deep, boss."

"Eat me."

Chapter 62

"Who called in this tip?" Ryan asked as he, Todd, and Stevens drove off in Todd's cruiser.

"Anonymous," Todd answered.

"Anonymous?"

"That's what I said."

"Okay, let's say you're telling the truth, how would anyone know we were looking for him?" Stevens asked.

"Your contingency plan?" Ryan said. "Todd, don't send us into a situation blind."

"All right, guys, you're right. I can't send you into anything without all the information," Todd started. "I told someone to keep an eye on him."

"So who called in the tip?" Ryan questioned.

"After the incident with Tayler, I reached out to a member of Sokolov's family, Seri's nephew."

"How the hell did you pull that off?" Stevens asked.

"I played him, worked his nerve about protecting his family. I told him if he gave me Brown, I'd make sure his uncle would stay out of the crossfire," Todd explained.

"So, you just told him to follow Brown around?"

"I didn't even have to do that. Joey is driving them right now, and will testify against Brown."

"Just got a text from Tayler—she found a witness, says she's willing to sit with a sketch artist," Ryan said, checking his phone.

"Have her take a statement and send a uniform to escort them to the station. I don't want Tayler to leave her side," Todd said.

"Where are we going?" Stevens asked.

"The docks."

"Why the docks? What's going on?"

"According to Joey, that's where Brown is meeting Sokolov. They will be at the same place, the perfect time to get them both."

"We'd have to be extremely careful to get the drop on them."

"That's where Joey comes in—you two get Brown, I get Sokolov, and Joey convinces his uncle to work with us."

"What about the other two? They aren't just gonna stand there," Ryan asked.

"I've got an arsenal in the trunk; we'll just simply have to outgun them," Todd replied.

Chapter 63

When we pulled up, Seri was there waiting on us with his arm around Natalya, but my attention wasn't on her. We weren't free just yet. We still needed to get paid.

"Who's the muscle?" John asked.

"He's new. I've only seen him around a handful of times," Joey replied. "He's actually your replacement."

We got out of the car, and as the three of us gathered what few things we had thrown in the trunk, Joey walked up and hugged his uncle.

"Something's off," John said in a low enough voice to where only the three of us could hear him.

"Just stay alert," I said as Seri walked toward us.

"Joey tells me the job is done."

"That's why we're here," I said, showing him a picture of the bodies from my cell phone.

"Outstanding," Seri said with a smile and excitement in his voice. "I trust there were no problems?"

"Has there ever been?"

"I would have to say no. So I guess this is it?"

"Yeah, this is it. We walk away, and you never have to see or hear from us again—after you pay us, of course," I said.

"Of course," Seri said as he motioned for his muscle to get a duffle bag from the back of his car, but before he got to the door, he froze.

"What's wrong?" Seri shouted.

"Someone's here."

"Drop the guns!"

Chapter 64

Before I could grab my gun, I felt one dig into my back. I could see that both John and Tony had their hands up to my right, and Seri's bodyguard had his hands behind his head.

"What the hell is this?" Seri shouted at me.

"You think this was us?"

"Well, well, well, look at this, Seri Sokolov, the major crime boss."

"Oh, I don't fucking believe this," I said when I realized who it was.

"And the man who does his dirty work, Zack Brown," Todd said as he cuffed Seri's muscle to the car and removed his weapons.

"Oh, this is just amazing. Stevens, is that you behind me?" I asked.

"Yeah, it's me."

"You've got to be loving this. How bad do you want to pull that trigger?"

"Shut up, Brown," Ryan said.

"How did you find us?" I asked. "There's no way we're that sloppy."

"No, you were actually very careful. I was just able to stay off your radar."

"Then how'd you make it here?" John asked again.

"When you were focusing all your attention on Seri, you left the back door wide open," Todd explained.

Everyone thought about that statement for a minute. I saw the guys turn and look at Joey, the only one who didn't have a gun pointed at him, and I kept my eyes on Seri. He had his nephew drive us so we wouldn't turn on him, only to have his own flesh and blood lead the cops to him.

"That wasn't your mother on the phone, was it?" Tony asked.

"His mother died years ago," Seri answered for him.

"That's a low even Seri wouldn't drop to," John said.

"Using your dead mother? That's just disrespectful," I added, trying to provoke Seri into trying something stupid.

"Damn the disrespect to his mother, he disrespected Seri's sister," John said.

"Joey, tell me this isn't true," Seri pleaded, trying not to listen to us.

"Seri, I had to, I had to make sure you were protected. Todd said if you cooperate, you'd stay out of jail," Joey said.

"And you trusted him?" I asked.

"That's a big risk, trusting an obsessed cop," Tony added.

"All right, that's enough. Everyone shut up," Todd said, trying to defuse the situation. "Seri, put your hands behind your back."

"You think you've got us beat?" John asked.

"You are getting arrested right now, and I don't think that you'll find a loophole out of this one," Todd answered. "So yeah, I believe I do."

"Well, I'd hate to go down without a fight," I said.

Chapter 65

I looked over my shoulder, and I could see that Ryan had Tony's hands already zip-tied behind his back, and he was starting to handcuff John, who wasn't going easily. I took a quick look at Todd. He was moving toward Seri, who was still standing in shock with his eyes on his nephew.

I took a deep breath and waited for Stevens to reach for my hands. I heard him holster his gun, and when I felt his fingers on my right wrist, I made my move.

As he pulled back my arm, I spun around and threw my left elbow into Stevens' temple, causing him to stagger backward. I tucked and rolled to the right of Stevens, toward my gun as a bullet flew into the car behind me. I sprang up and fired a shot at Ryan, who still wasn't able to get John cuffed, catching him in his left leg. The shock of a gunshot wound caused him to fall to the ground, dropping his gun and grabbing his injury with both of his hands.

"Cut Tony loose!" I shouted as I took cover behind the sedan that brought us to this trap.

I peered over the trunk and saw John pulling Tony behind the car to my left to take refuge. Once there, John cut off the zip ties and handed him a gun. Straight ahead of me, I saw Todd tackle Seri to the ground. They fought for a moment, but Seri was able to knock Todd's gun away, causing them to disengage and take cover. Behind them, Seri's bodyguard was able to reach into the glove compartment and find a spare gun to join the fight. I fired a few shots at them, both of which struck the car they arrived in.

I ducked back down to reload and, luckily, saw Ryan reaching for his gun again. I shouted at Tony, trying to get his attention; however, over the gunfire, they couldn't hear me. I took a knee, aimed, and fired two armor-piercing rounds into Ryan's chest.

No hesitation. Any later, my two best friends would have been dead. Ryan stared at me the entire time until the weight of his lifeless body was flat on the ground. I honestly think that's the first time I'd actually seen the lights go out in a person.

Chapter 66

"Ryan!" Todd shouted. As Todd rushed to his detective's aid, John and Tony ran to join me in the little cover the sedan offered.

Todd slid into Ryan, grabbing him by the shoulders and shaking him frantically, trying to get his fallen detective to wake up; when that didn't work, he began CPR. After roughly a minute, the realization that Ryan was gone set in. Todd bent down, hugged his body, apologized to him, then turned and opened fire on us.

"You son of a bitch!"

"You brought this on yourself, Greg. Don't blame me for collateral damage."

"You will pay for this," he said after firing a few more shots.

From behind me, I could hear Stevens start to move. He had started crawling and was reaching for his weapon.

"Don't do it, Stevens," Tony said, pointing a gun at him.

"I'm through taking orders from you," he answered.

Stevens looked at Todd, who was shaking his head, basically begging him to stand down.

"Drop the gun, Jerry."

"I'm sorry, sir. I have to do this."

"Jerry, don't!" Todd shouted.

But it was too late. Stevens grabbed his gun and fired a shot out of desperation. The bullet hit Tony in the thigh, dropping him to one knee, screaming in pain. After Tony fell, John grabbed him from under both of his arms and dragged him to the car so he could lean against it.

Now we were really in a tight spot. We had Todd on one side shooting at us, and on the other side, there was Stevens doing the same thing.

We were able to stay out of Todd's line of sight, which abled John to help keep pressure on Tony's leg. I rose up and took a shot at Todd, who was ducked down behind his cruiser, then turned and fired at Stevens to keep him at bay.

"How is he?"

"He's losing a lot of blood. We gotta get him outta here."

"All right, I'll lay down cover fire, get him in the back, and we'll haul ass," I said as I reloaded.

I shot two rounds at Stevens, who had managed to take cover behind a pile of empty wooden pallets and then fired two rounds at Todd.

"Nut up, T, this might hurt," John said as he lifted Tony up into the car.

I turned to get in, and just as I opened the door, two bullets struck it, just missing me. I turned around and saw Stevens running to join his captain as he fired. That was it, I snapped. I didn't see anything but Detective Jerry Stevens, and I knew I had to kill him. I emptied the clip of my .9 mm into his back.

"No! Goddammit!" Todd screamed.

"Again, this is on you!" I shouted back.

"I will kill you. You hear me, Zack, I will kill you!"

"Why don't you let me take care of that?" a voice said from behind me.

I heard a gunshot, and the last thing I remember was John firing multiple shots and grabbing me, trying to pick me up. Then, it was just dark.

Chapter 67

"So, after a week, I.A. has turned up nothing?"

"That's correct. Honestly, sir, I don't think there's anything to turn up."

"There are three things that are certain in this life. Death, taxes, and there is always a reason."

"A reason, sir?"

"There's a reason that two of our detectives are in a cooler with bullet holes in them. And as mayor of this city, it's my obligation to find out why."

Mayor Christopher Sullivan was a Marine veteran, where he was awarded a Purple Heart after his second tour in the Gulf War. When he came home, he spent 20 years on the force, working his way up to sergeant, before making the jump to politics. It was believed he would be making a move to governor, maybe even Senate in the next few years.

"All the evidence collected points to a gunfight, and our guys were just in the wrong place at the wrong time."

"There's more to it. I can feel it. Have we found out what case they were on?"

"From what I can tell, they were assigned a few cold cases and had been chasing old leads for the past few days."

"In my experience, cold cases don't lead to gun battles at the docks."

"What should we do then?"

"Get Todd in here," Sullivan said after thinking about it. "I want to question him myself."

Chapter 68

Two weeks had passed since Todd lost his two detectives, and he wasn't handling it well. Every single night, when he lay down to sleep, Ryan's and Stevens' faces were the last things he saw.

"How are you, Greg?" the mayor asked.

"Lately, I've been taking my life one bottle at a time."

"That's not healthy at all."

"What the fuck else am I supposed to do?"

"You seem to be taking a lot of guilt over this."

"Two of my best are meat popsicles because of a case I assigned them. How am I supposed to feel?"

"I suppose you're right, so let's just cut to the chase," Sullivan said.

The mayor was focused on one thing, the truth. And as cold as it was, he was willing to push Todd as far as he had to, to get to it.

"Why am I here?" Todd asked.

"Because, I'm launching an investigation into you, Detective Stevens, and Detective Ryan," Sullivan answered.

"Excuse me?" Todd asked. "What about them?"

"I'm just a little confused. Why were they at the docks?" the mayor asked.

"They were following a lead."

"Care to elaborate on that?"

"You've got the file, the evidence, what more do you want to know?"

"For starters, how about the case they were working?"

"They were looking into some unsolved murders. When they came across some intel that connected them to Zack Brown, I had them tail him for a few days."

"So that's what's going on here," Sullivan said with the preverbal light bulb going off above his head. "Still chasing that ghost?"

"He's not a ghost," Todd said. "At least he wasn't."

"What do you mean *he wasn't*?"

"After he killed my detectives, his boss, Seri Sokolov, put two rounds in his back."

"Wait a damn minute. Brown works for Sokolov?" Sullivan asked. Even at his pay grade, the mayor had no clue how good we were.

"Saw it with my own eyes. Stevens even confirmed it."

"How the hell did a probie like Stevens find out?" Sullivan asked. The fact that a rookie detective made a break that big in a case that had haunted Todd's career before he or Ryan, the precinct's head detective, could, piqued his interest.

Todd thought about that for a second. What was he supposed to do here? He realized how Stevens must have felt when he assigned him the case. He was truly between a rock and a hard place. He knew he had to protect his men.

"Well?" the mayor asked.

"I have no idea," he started. "He must have seen something I missed."

"You know every single line in that file. You expect me to believe that he found something that you overlooked?"

"That's what my report is going to say."

Chapter 69

"Seri darling, don't you think it's time to go home?" Natalya asked.

Seri had taken her and his two best bodyguards to a safe house in upstate New York while the heat died down. He was still reeling from the fact that his own nephew turned on him.

"C'mon baby; it's been two weeks, how bad can it be?" she continued.

That was a question Seri really couldn't answer. He had been in this house for two weeks, basically just trying to accept the fact that he couldn't even trust his family, and to make things worse, he had started to think he'd made a mistake.

"I don't know yet, love. I can't guarantee your safety," he finally said.

"Guarantee it or not, I'm leaving. Call me when you grow a set."

"Wait, wait, wait," Seri said just before she got to the door. "What if I send these two out to check the house, and we have a night alone?"

"One night?" Natalya said.

"Every night, if they say the loft is clear."

"I hate you," she said. "One more night here, but after that, I will leave you."

"You won't have to," Seri replied. "Boys, go check the house. And if you see Joey, kill him."

Chapter 70

"Even if your report says that, what about the physical evidence?" Sullivan asked as he drank his coffee.

"Physical evidence?"

"Yes, the physical evidence, as in the evidence we collected at the scene. You claim that Brown was shot twice in the back by Sokolov, correct?"

"Yes, sir."

"There are two problems with that story."

"And what would they be?" Todd asked.

"There is no evidence, physical or otherwise, that points to Sokolov even being there," Sullivan explained.

"Sir, you can't believe that. Pull the rounds from Brown's back, and I'll guarantee that they'll match Sokolov's personal handgun," Todd pleaded.

"I'm glad you said that because it brings us to the second problem," Sullivan said.

"And what is that?"

"The second problem is that there is no body."

"Excuse me?"

"Brown's body was never recovered."

"Sir, that's not possible. I saw him get shot, and without help, there's no way he could've survived," Todd said.

"And his team?" Sullivan asked.

"What about them?"

"Well, if they're as good as you say they are, it wouldn't be a problem for them to patch their leader up."

"They aren't that smart."

"Aren't they?" the mayor questioned.

Chapter 71

"Have you ever seen the boss put in his place like that?"

"Wanna know an unspoken truth?"

"What's that?"

"We don't work for Seri. Natalya actually runs the family."

"Get the fuck outta here."

"Think about it. You know that old saying, happy wife, happy life?"

Seri's two bodyguards joked and bullshitted until they reached the loft. They gave it a good once over, checking every room, closet, garage, back alley, and under the beds. Once they decided it was clear, they called their boss to see what the next move would be.

"Let's go. Boss wants us back to escort them."

"Outstanding."

They locked up the loft and started heading back to the car. Just before they got in to drive off, one of them caught a glimpse of a silver Ultima parked on the opposite side of the street about halfway up the street.

"Wait a minute; you see that?"

"That looks a lot like the car that was parked outside the safe house. Coincidence?"

"Not likely—call Seri now."

Chapter 72

Ever had that feeling that you're falling and when you're just about to hit the ground, your body jolts and you wake up? I believe it's called a myoclonic jerk? That's how I woke up.

Once I caught my breath, I started looking around the room. The walls were a dull white color with nothing hanging on them. In fact, the only thing in the room was the bed I was lying on and a table with a clock on it.

12:18 pm.

"What happened? We didn't get to the docks till past 8–8:30 pm," I said to myself. "Think. What do you remember? Stevens running away, I shot him. Then *I* got shot."

I slowly got out of the bed, trying not to hurt myself any more than I already was. I reached behind me, which caused me to lean forward in pain, and felt a bandage on my lower back, and as I straightened up, I felt another one a little higher up.

"Shot twice?" I wondered. Being shot is the worst feeling ever. Trust me when I say that. Every single move you make hurts; you never realize how much you have to use muscles until they have holes in them.

I started to walk to the door, to continue looking around, and just before I reached for the doorknob, I felt a tug that came with very sharp pain.

"Oh, you have got to be kidding me. First, I get shot, and now there's a mother fucking catheter in me? This is not going to be a good day."

I found the bathroom and, after a few excruciatingly painful minutes, pulled out the catheter before continuing to explore further.

Chapter 73

There were pictures along the wall of a woman and her family, none of which I recognized. Counting the room I was in, this was maybe a three-bedroom, two baths, probably a two-income middle-class home. I took a look inside the second bedroom and was surprised at what I saw. There were *Batman* action figures and *Justice League* sheets on the bed—more than likely, a room for a young boy.

As I got closer to the open space at the end of the hall, I could hear sports broadcasters calling a soccer match, Ireland vs. France. That only meant one person could be in that room, John. I've never been so happy to hear that Irish bastard. He was just sitting on the couch, beer in hand, yelling at the TV.

"Who's winning?"

"Zacky?" he said, turning around. "How do you feel?"

"Like I've been shot."

"Here, let me help you. You shouldn't be moving around so much."

"Oh, shut up," I said as I gradually took a seat. "I shouldn't have had a catheter in me."

"That wasn't my idea," John said. "You need anything to eat or drink? Wanna shot?"

"No, I'm fine," I said. "Why did I have a catheter in me anyway?"

"Nobody wanted to volunteer to change your diaper."

"What the hell are you talking about?" I asked. "I haven't wet the bed since I was like three years old. I think I would've made it just fine."

"Boss, you were out for close to two weeks."

Chapter 74

Hearing that made me speechless; I just stared at John, trying to process what I just heard. There's no way that could be the truth. I couldn't have been in a coma, not me. I was always the one who just got flesh wounds, bumps, and bruises, that kind of stuff. I always thought if anything, I'd go out with a bang, but now I realize that maybe I'm really not bulletproof.

"Wanna run that by me again?" I finally said.

"Yeah, I know how that must sound," he started. "You've been asleep for a while."

"How is that even possible?"

"After you were shot, you fell forward and slammed your head on the bumper of the car."

"That explains the bump on my forehead."

"After you went down, I tried to see if you could walk, but your eyes were just glazed over. I threw you into the car, and we got the hell out of there."

"How'd we end up here? Where is here, anyway?"

"You lost a lot of blood. And with all the attention brought on by the cops, we couldn't just walk into a hospital. We were able to stop the bleeding, but one of the bullets was deep."

"So how did you get it out?"

"We didn't."

"I knew it; I died, didn't I?"

"Came close, very damn close, but no, you're not dead yet."

"All right, John, spill it."

"Zack, don't overreact, Brian patched you up."

Chapter 75

"Please tell me you did not just say what I heard you say."

"Calm down. We had no other choice."

"You could've figured something out," I said. I was furious. It took time and effort to get Brian into hiding, and now we were dragging him right back out.

"We tried to patch you up, but we just couldn't. We didn't know what else to do."

"You could've left me out in front of the ER, convince a vet to do emergency surgery, drive to a different burrow, for God's sake."

"You don't think we tried that?" John shouted. "We could barely get out of the city. The gunfight had sirens going off everywhere, and on top of that, we had to be aware of Natano's crew."

"Then you should've left me there."

"Like you would've left one of us?"

He had a point, and it was actually one I couldn't argue. There's no way in hell I would've let one of them die, not without first doing everything short of making a deal with the devil, and even that wasn't out of the question.

"So, where are we?" I asked, looking around the house. We had to be up in the country; there was a backyard.

"Portland, Maine."

"Maine?"

"I'll let Brian explain that one."

"And where is he, anyway?"

"He and Tony went out to get food and some more medical crap for you."

"Come at me with another cock probe, and I'll kill all three of you myself," I said, leaning back into the couch.

Chapter 76

John and I sat and watched the game, only breaking our silence to cheer for what helped our team and to wish death on the official when he made a call against us. It was about 45 minutes before Tony and Brian made it back, and it was clear that they were not expecting to see me up and moving.

"Wow, you're up?" Tony said.

"Don't sound so excited."

"Just unexpected; how are you feeling?"

"I'm fine, just wondering which one of you I'm going to slap for putting a catheter in me," I said.

"It had to be done. You look good, man," Brian said.

Those were the first words I'd heard Brian say in almost three years. It was surreal seeing him standing there. He looked like he'd aged 20 years. Last I saw him, he was fit and clean-shaven with a crew cut. Now he's got shaggy hair and a full beard with grey starting to show.

"Tony was trying to get me caught up on everything that's happened," Brian started. "You really asked to get out?"

"Yeah, sure did," I said in an aggravated tone.

"Ballsy, even for you, what went wrong?"

"They haven't told you?"

"We've been a little busy keeping you alive," Brian answered.

"We were blindsided," John started.

"I'm sorry, but I have to talk to you," I said as I looked straight at Brian. I couldn't hold back anymore; I had to speak my mind.

"Zack, we called him," John said.

"And we'll deal with that in a minute."

Chapter 77

Brian and I, limping but determined, went out to the backyard where I was surprised to see how much it resembled the porch at home. A couple of chairs, a cooler all lit up with a dull yellow light. If you took away the manicured grass, trampoline, bicycles, and add the sounds of the city, it was the exact replica. I wondered if Brian had done that on purpose.

"You wanna go first, or should I?"

"Zack, I know what you're gonna say."

"I don't care; I'm going to say it anyway," I said, cutting him off. "You know what we went through, getting you out?"

"Yeah, Boss, I know. And I'm forever in your debt for what you did for my family."

"You don't owe us a damn thing. We did it *because* you are our family. And we'd do it again. I only gave you one stipulation—stay hidden," I said, taking a deep breath as it was getting harder to breathe.

"Calm down, brother, you're not 100 percent yet, you've got to take it easy."

"I'll calm down when I'm damn good and ready," I said, taking a seat. "You still owe me an explanation."

"First off, I'm still hidden. We're in Maine."

"And? People could still find you."

"Not when everyone, including you, think my alias lives in Utah."

He had me there. I set up a fake name, bank account, social security, everything anyone could think of and had the address set up to a P.O. Box in Salt Lake.

"Second, if I were the one who was fighting for their life, you would've been on the first plane, train, boat, or whatever you could find to make your way to help me."

The bastard had made another valid point. Brian was always there for me, and I was there for him. But that's not why I was mad; it was something else.

"Where are Shawna and Alyx?"

Brian paused for a few seconds trying to find the right words before just coming right out and saying it.

"Dallas."

"What?" I asked, dumbfounded.

"You heard me."

"How could you let that happen?"

"It's not what you think. My friends needed help, and I wanted them safe," he said.

I had never felt more thankful to have a friend like that and never felt more like an ass.

Chapter 78

Shawna had met Brian one weekend about four years ago at the New York Aquarium, and that's all it took; Brian was in love. I knew when Shawna got pregnant, we had to get him out.

"Does she know what's going on?"

"To an extent, she knows about my past and has made her peace with it," he said. "All I told her was that you were shot and needed my help."

"You have an amazing woman."

I truly meant that. Shawna was a jewel. She was a great cook, a wonderful mother, and was making a name for herself pursuing a career in medicine.

"Tell her thanks. I know your clumsy ass didn't learn to do a patch job alone," I said as I stood up and gave Brian a long overdue hug, and then the two of us headed inside.

John had his back to us as we walked in, and I made it a point to give him a good smack on the back of his head. As I walked around the table, I made sure to do the same thing to Tony, who was shuffling cards.

"Guess we got off easy," John said, looking at Tony.

"I'll take it," he replied.

"I owe you guys," I said.

"You would've done the same for us," John said.

"Hey, at least we're out," Tony said as he started dealing.

"We're not out yet," I answered.

"What do you mean?"

"Who was the last person to take a shot at any of us, and was lucky enough to connect, that's still alive?"

"Yeah, but Zacky, the police have all our faces posted up, and probably have half the damn force looking for us," John said.

"Not to mention that if the cops haven't already, Seri and his new crew probably have eyes on every one of our safe houses," Tony added.

"Well, there are four of us now, we're better this way," I started. "Not to mention, we have one great advantage."

"What's that?" Tony asked.

"Everyone thinks I'm dead."

Chapter 79

"We may have a problem."

"Excuse me?" Seri answered. That was not a phrase he wanted to hear right now.

"It might be nothing, but we spotted a car outside the loft, looks like the one that was outside the safe house."

"That's impossible. Nobody knows where this place is."

"I don't know, pretty sure it's the same car."

"Well, let's not jump to any conclusions. Get the plate number and see if it tails you. Be sure to check the block when you get back," Seri said as he hung up the phone.

"Problem?" Natalya asked as she handed him a martini.

"Not really sure."

"I'm not staying here any longer," she started.

"For once, just shut up," Seri snapped. He had grown tired of her constant nagging.

"Excuse me?"

"I said, shut up," he repeated. "I'm trying to keep us safe, and I'm sick of you doing nothing but bitch."

"A real man wouldn't have to try. A real man would strike down any man who crossed him," she screamed.

Seri raised his right hand and swung it across Natalya's face, landing on her right cheek with a loud slap. Her head turned, and she instinctively put her hands over her face. Seri had never struck her before. He'd always composed himself and never let her see his emotions.

"You watch your fucking mouth. From now on, you will treat me with the respect I deserve."

Seri had snapped. The stress of dealing with a high maintenance girlfriend, the realization of his family turning on him, and now the thought of being followed was just too much.

"When the guys get back, we'll evaluate the situation, and then decide what we will do."

Chapter 80

"So, we don't know where Brown is?" Todd asked.

"I've got teams searching the floor of the river in case they dumped him," the mayor answered.

"There's no chance. Even if Zack didn't make it, they'd never just leave him."

"No matter, we've got checkpoints set up across the city. Every vehicle is getting searched," Sullivan said.

"We'll find them," the mayor's assistant, Ramirez, said.

"With all due respect, you're a fucking *Yes-Man*. You don't know a damn thing," Todd said.

"Excuse me?" the newly dubbed *Yes-Man* asked. "Your report describes a gunfight, correct?"

"Your words, but yes."

"Wouldn't a few rounds naturally hit one of the cars that were there? One of the cars they took cover behind, maybe?" the Yes-Man asked in a condescending tone.

"Well, let's think about that," Todd started. "You've just shot and killed two cops in a shootout. Would you keep a car that was rattled with bullets? One that could be easily picked out by any witnesses or survivors?"

The Yes-Man, realizing that he hadn't fully thought the scenario through, stood to refill his coffee cup.

"Wait a minute," Todd said. "How soon did you get the checkpoints up?"

"Within an hour, maybe an hour and a half," Sullivan answered.

"That's why you haven't found them."

"You think they made it out of the city, with two of them shot and one badly wounded?" Ramirez asked.

"If I have to tell you one more time that nobody, I mean nobody, knows them better than me, I will shoot you."

"Now, wait a minute," Sullivan started. "You know Brown inside and out, but if he's not around anymore, who's to say what the other two would do?"

"Trust me, if, and that's a big if, Brown is gone, John and Tony are just as dangerous, if not more."

"Why more?" Sullivan asked.

"Because now they're mad and more than likely they're going to be out for revenge," Todd said. "And with no Zack around to call the shots, I wouldn't be surprised at anything John and Tony do."

"First name basis?"

Chapter 81

After what seemed like days, there was a knock at the door followed by three more—the signal Seri had designated for situations like this.

"What the fuck took you so long?" Seri asked.

"We took a few extra turns to see if we were being tailed."

"And?"

"We were followed for a few blocks, but we lost them."

"Could you tell who was driving?"

"No, they had tinted windows and stayed back just far enough that we couldn't see."

"Where did you lose them?" Seri asked.

"About ten minutes after we left the loft."

Seri took a minute to think. He wanted to go home just as bad as Natalya but knew it would be safer to stay hidden for at least a few more days. He took a glance over at Natalya, who was still shaken over the fact that he'd actually struck her. She refused to make eye contact with him. Instead, she just stared a hole into the wall.

"What do you think we should do?"

"Whoever was following you obviously wants to know who's at the loft," Seri started. "We'll head that way, but if we see that same car again, we stop."

"Stop?"

"And then we'll see who it is that's just so interested in the loft," Seri finished as he tucked his gun into his waist.

"Who do you think it is?"

"It's a toss-up between the cops and Natano's crew if I had to guess. You coming or what?" he asked Natalya.

"Shut up; I'm coming," she said as she brushed past him.

Chapter 82

Todd sat silently in his chair, looking at the mayor, who was waiting on his answer. He now knew exactly how Stevens felt when he assigned him the last case of his life.

"Had to come out eventually," Todd started. "I grew up with them."

"Well, isn't that interesting," Sullivan said.

"Not really, I'm sure you grew up with friends too."

"Not ones that I led investigations into."

"It does raise some questions," Ramirez said.

"Such as?"

"Well, for starters, it sheds some light as to why they've never been caught."

"You think I'd betray the badge like that?" Todd asked.

"I think you've got to convince us otherwise, and given everything we know, that won't be easy," Ramirez said with a smirk.

"If it wasn't for me, this department would have a stack of unsolved murders with no viable suspect."

"That's enough," Sullivan said. "I highly doubt a man with such a career as Captain Greg Todd has put together, that he'd jeopardize it by aiding and abetting."

"Thank you, sir."

"However, if you did contribute to Brown's involvement in any of those unsolved, you'll spend the rest of your days banging a metal cup against bars."

"So, what's our next move?" Ramirez asked.

"We need to find out if Brown survived," Todd said.

"I'll have some people look into it," Sullivan said. "In the meantime, I need you to tell me everything you know about Brown."

Todd ran his fingers through his hair and rubbed his bloodshot eyes. He stared at the pile of papers, just trying to get his thoughts in order.

"Wait a minute," he said, thinking back.

"What is it?"

"There used to be four."

"What do you mean?"

"Four of them, Brown plus three," Todd explained.

Chapter 83

Seri followed Natalya down the stairs and through the alley that ran alongside the building. She was walking with a purpose, trying to show Seri that he hadn't rattled her. Her heels were hitting the ground with such force that it was drowning out the sounds of the city. She swung open the back door and took her seat behind the passenger seat. Seri popped the trunk, and one of his henchmen dropped in a load of overnight bags.

"Take the same route you took this morning," Seri started. "Just remember that if you see that car, stop."

"Yes, sir."

"Put the partition up," Seri said as he opened his door.

The car started and drove away from the safe house, minding the rules of the road, drawing as little attention as possible. They turned about every two to three blocks to ensure that there wasn't a tail on them, also causing a very frustrating drive for the ravishing Russian and her salty companion.

"You need to learn your place," Seri said, breaking the silence.

"What did you just say?" Natalya said with disgust in her voice.

"I'm done with you second-guessing everything I do. You will start respecting and obeying me, do you understand?"

"You know the difference between you and your father?"

"My father isn't here, so I don't give a damn what the difference is."

Natalya was staring at him with rage in her eyes when suddenly there was a tap on the partition glass, and it rolled down.

"Seri, that's the car."

"We'll finish this later," Seri said to Natalya. "Rear-end them."

"What?"

"Rear-end them, now!" Seri yelled. "When he stops, both of you rush the car and pull that fucker out; I'll handle it from there."

The car started speeding up and swerving in and out of traffic until it was right behind the car that's caused Seri so much stress the past few hours. Just as they got in front of the loft, smash.

The car rocked to a stop. The windshield was cracked, the hood bent all the way up to a point, and smoke was pouring out of the engine block.

"Go," Seri ordered.

He waited until he saw both his guys at the front of the car before he got out. As Seri opened his door, Natalya grabbed his arm and looked straight into his heartless eyes.

"If you ever lay a hand on me again, I'll cut your balls off and stuff them down your throat."

Chapter 84

Seri's henchmen ran to the front of the car, with their guns drawn.

"Don't fucking move!" one shouted as the driver door began to open.

"Don't shoot," a voice called out.

"You've got to be kidding me."

"What is it?" Seri asked as he reached for his gun.

"You won't believe this."

"Oh wow, look who finally grew a set. Get him inside and tie him to a chair," Seri said, tucking his gun back into his pants.

"Seri, please, no."

"Shut up!" Seri screamed as he smacked him across the face. As soon as Seri hit him, it triggered something, something scary.

Seri began swinging wildly at him, not caring where or how hard his hands struck until finally, he stopped and started walking back to his car.

"Get him upstairs!" Seri shouted again.

One of his bodyguards grabbed the driver and tossed him over his shoulders and started heading up the stairs to the loft; the other followed Seri back toward their town car to retrieve Natalya. When Seri opened the back door and reached for her hand, she wasn't there.

"Where the hell is she?"

"I don't know; I didn't see her get out."

"Fuck!" Seri shouted out in frustration. "You go find her, and I'll deal with this crap."

Chapter 85

"There's never been any evidence of a fourth," Ramirez said.

"There is barely any evidence of the first three," Todd replied. "It's been a long time since I've even thought of him."

"Who is the fourth?" Sullivan asked.

"Brian Wilkerson. They used to call him Bdub. He was a good guy, loyal to a fault," Todd explained.

"What do you mean *used to* and *was a good guy*?"

"Last I heard, he died about three years ago, give or take."

"If he's dead, why even bring him up?" Sullivan asked.

"It's complicated."

"I don't give a damn how complicated it is; you're going to tell me every single thing you know," Sullivan said.

Todd sat there and thought carefully about his next words would be. He had been lying for so long that it was hard to remember what he had told to whom. The last thing he wanted to do was to get caught up in his own lie.

"A lot of what I know is just rumors," Todd said as he stood up to readjust himself. "But it never seemed to fit until now."

"Spit it out, man."

Todd took a breath and started to try and think of a way to explain what he knew without revealing his dark past.

"Look, these guys have probably used dozens of false identities. They could've easily made one of them disappear."

"You think they just gave this guy a new ID and parted ways?" Sullivan asked.

"He isn't just a random guy they hired. He was a friend since grade school," Todd answered.

"How do you know that?" Ramirez asked.

"All in due time," Todd answered. "But one thing I know for sure is that the only way to get away from the family is death."

"Fake a death, then?"

"It's the only thing that makes sense," Todd said.

"So now the real question is, how do we find a ghost?"

The three men sat in their respective chairs and wondered what their next move was. How do you start looking for someone when nobody even really knows if you're alive?

"We don't," Todd finally said. "We wait for him to come to us."

"What do you mean?"

"Regardless if they're out of the family or not, regardless if they're wounded, they'll be out for revenge," Todd said. "So, all we have to do is sit back and wait."

"I will not have a war in my city," Sullivan said.

"Absolutely not, we just watch the person they'll be coming after."

"Sokolov."

"And as soon as they show, we take them down."

Chapter 86

"Tie him in that chair," Seri said as they walked into his loft.

Seri was still fuming as he pulled off his jacket and watched as his second in command carried out his order.

"What are we gonna do with him?"

"I'm going to kill him," Seri responded.

"Please, please, let me explain."

"Maybe we should let him."

Seri thought about it for a few seconds. No matter what was said, it wasn't going to change his mind. However, he felt like he owed him that much.

"All right, Joey, explain your side. Please tell me why you turned your back on your own family," Seri said.

"I was trying to protect you," Joey said, still trying to catch his breath.

"Protect me?" Seri shouted as he slapped Joey in the face. "I'm Seri Sokolov! I don't need a piss ant like you to protect me."

"You don't understand," Joey pleaded, still coughing up blood. "He knew things."

"Wait a minute," Seri said, taking a seat in front of his beaten nephew. "What are you talking about? Did you let Brown get to you?"

"No. Brown didn't get to me. I know all of his tricks," Joey started. "It was Todd. Greg Todd."

"What the fuck did you just say?" Seri asked in disbelief.

Chapter 87

Seri was just staring blankly at his nephew. Now it was all starting to come together; the cops weren't following Brown, they were following Joey. What didn't make sense is why now? How much did Todd actually know?

"So the cops came to you and said what? That I was in danger?"

"No, he contacted me and told me that he was close to proving that Brown worked for the family," Joey said with his head hung, still trying to catch his breath.

"That's impossible," Seri said as he stood up. "He is lying to you, dumbass, trying to rattle your cage."

"No, no, he had information that backed up everything that he said. I don't know where he got it from."

"You've put me in a tough spot here, Joe."

"Seri, I was trying to protect you."

"I don't need protection from anyone, especially from the people who want to see my empire burn!" Seri shouted.

"I'm sorry, I'm so sorry."

"I'm sorry too, Joe, but you've left me no choice," Seri said as he pointed his gun at him.

"Seri, no, please," Joey begged. "I'm family."

"You stopped being family when you talked to the cops."

Seri paused for a minute as Joey began to cry and beg for his life. He closed his eyes, said a prayer in Russian, then fired three bullets into his nephew's chest.

"Wrap him in the rug," Seri said as he pushed the coffee table aside with his foot. "Drop him someplace public, at a park or something."

"You sure?"

"He deserves to be buried with some dignity."

"You got it, boss."

"Make it fast; we need to find Natalya. I've got another bullet left for her."

Chapter 88

I was sitting at the kitchen table with a beer in front of me, just staring into space. I could hear Brian and John watching TV, just bullshitting back and forth. Tony walked out of the bathroom and said something to me that didn't even register.

"Zack?" he said, snapping his fingers in front of me. "You with us, buddy?"

"What?" I said, coming back to earth.

"You all right, man?"

"Yeah, sorry, I zoned out for a minute."

"What's on your mind?"

"Sokolov, I want him dead."

"I know. Don't worry, man, we'll get him."

"He's got to be in hiding," I said, rubbing my eyes.

"Well, we know where his safe house is, seems pretty straight forward."

"Damn, it's super serious in here," Brian said as he and John came in for refills. "What are you guys talking about?"

"Zack's planning his revenge," Tony said.

"Glad to see that you're back," John said. "You sure you're ready?"

That question put a look on my face that needed no words. John simply put his hands in the air and took a seat next to Tony at the table.

"So, what do you have so far?" Brian asked.

"Look, Brian, I appreciate you patching me up and letting us hide out here, but this is our problem."

"The fuck it is. Whether you like it or not, I'm a part of this now. You three are family, so let's end this for good."

There was nothing I could say. It would be pointless to argue with him because he wouldn't back down; hell, he's more stubborn than I am. Plus, he could be helpful to have around in case anything went sideways.

"We think the best place to start looking is his safe house," Tony said, breaking the silence.

"Why there?" Brian asked.

"The cops are most likely sitting on his loft, and he'd want to stay off their radar for a while," John answered.

"But Joey was working with Todd. He could've easily told him about Seri's safe house," I said.

"Joe flipped?" Brian asked. "What the hell is going on out there?"

"Welcome to our world."

"So if we assume the cops know about the safe house, where does that leave us?" Tony asked.

"We could track his car," John said. "We know what he drives and most of his routes."

"We could make that work, ambush him at a stoplight or a parking garage, something like that," I said.

"That could get messy," Tony said with concern.

"I don't care. We're already out, and two of us are six feet under as far as he's concerned. Let's end this."

"What about Todd?"

Chapter 89

That was the million-dollar question. Todd had been a pain in my ass for years. He was constantly making it harder and harder for me to do my job. On the other hand, he was a good friend once upon a time.

"I think it's pretty obvious that he's not going to stop," John said.

"Yeah, but after everything that's happened, does he even have a badge anymore?" Brian asked.

"He followed his gut as any good cop would. I'm sure this wasn't the first time that he used extreme measures to close a case," I said.

"But I'd bet that this was the first time it blew up in his face," Tony added.

"So again, the question is, what do we do?"

"We wait," I said.

"Wait for what?"

"Until he gives us no choice. His world is about to come crashing down around him. Every secret he's ever had is about to be exposed. We may not need to do anything," I explained.

"What happens if it goes the other way?" John asked. "Are you going to be able to do what needs to be done?"

"We'll cross that bridge when we come to it," I said. Honestly, I had no idea if I'd be able to do it or not. Of course, this wouldn't be the first time I pulled a trigger out of revenge, but this is the first time the bullet would hit a friend.

"Zack, he's not going to stop. If you can't pull the trigger, I will."

"I know you will, Johnny. Let's get our shit together."

Chapter 90

Todd was sitting at his desk, reading over his incident report, trying to make sense of what had happened that night. His hands began to tremble as he thought about his fallen officers. He had lost people in the line of duty before, but not like this. His eyes began to water, and just as he reached for his bottle of scotch, there was a knock at his door.

"Sir, there's somebody here to see you."

"It's really not a good time," Todd said as he poured himself a drink.

"I know it's not, sir, but trust me, you wanna hear this."

"All right, fine, send them in," he said as he downed his drink and put the glass and bottle back in the bottom drawer.

"Inspector Todd?"

"What's left of him anyway—what can I do for you?"

"I need your help."

"With all due respect, ma'am, I just lost two officers and, not to be rude, but there is a whole police station out there," Todd said, pointing his finger out of his office door. "Why'd you ask for me?"

"Seri Sokolov wants me dead."

"What did you just say?" Todd said, snapping his head around to make eye contact.

"I'm in danger, and I need your help."

"How did you find me?" Todd continued to question.

"I hear things."

"You hear things?"

"Like how you've spent a large portion of your career chasing a man that there is very little evidence of if any. And most of it is off the record most likely because of a childhood friendship."

"You've got my attention."

"One way or the other, I'm disappearing. It'll either be on my own or with your help," the stranger said.

"Okay, I'll help you," Todd said after a few minutes of silence. "But first, I need to know who you are."

"I have your word that I'll be safe?"

"Yes, ma'am. You tell me everything you know, and I'll personally put you into Witness Protection."

The stranger nodded, pulled off her sunglasses, fedora, and wig. As soon as she did, Todd's eyes widened as he realized who he had been talking to.

"Natalya?"

"Now you understand why I need to disappear, yes?"

"Yeah, it's starting to make sense. What I don't understand is why he's coming after you?"

"Seri is losing control of everything. Ever since he put out the hit on Natano, he's been different. Making moves without thinking about the consequences. He snapped at me, hit me, and threatened me, so I left. In his current state, there's no telling what he'll do now."

Chapter 91

Seri was sitting in his love seat, staring out the window watching the city lights flicker in the night. He tried calling Natalya a dozen times with no luck—straight to voice mail every time.

"Where the fuck did you go?" he asked, looking at her picture on his phone.

The longer he sat in that chair, the more his anger grew. His fist was clenched as he started to dial Natalya's number for the last time. It rang once, twice, a third, and by the fourth, he was foaming at the mouth. When he heard the voice mail beep again, he lost it.

"You stupid bitch! No one leaves me! You're dead, you understand me? Dead!" Seri shouted into his phone. He flipped it close, then reared back and sent it flying through his window.

He continued to scream and shout in Russian as he started to trash the loft. Flipping over furniture and breaking mirrors, pictures, punching holes in the walls, until Ivan, his right-hand man, came busting through the door with his gun drawn.

"What the hell is going on? Are you all right?" Ivan asked as he took a look around.

"I'm fine," Seri grunted. "Put that away."

"Sorry, boss, with all the noise, I thought maybe something was going down," he said as he tucked his gun back into his jacket.

"I'm fine," Seri repeated.

"Yeah, I can see that," Ivan said as he kicked around some of the debris that lay on the ground. "I laid Joe on a bench in Central Park. Put the rug in a trash can behind a bar a few blocks away."

"Good, someone should find him any minute now."

"You sure that's a good thing? A dead body brings a lot of attention."

"He deserves to be laid to rest, not to be tossed out like trash," Seri said as he rubbed his eyes. "I owe his mother that much."

"I still think it's a bad idea. When the cops find him, it'll only be a matter of time before they come looking for you."

"We weren't the only people there. Brown's team could've just as easily been looking for revenge. We dump the gun, and it just gets traced back to itself if anyone finds it."

"We need to dump it across town. No sense in making it easy on them," Ivan said. "Now, where do we start looking for Natalya?"

"She's not answering her phone."

"Did you expect her to?"

"She's on the run. It won't be easy to find her. She's probably changed her appearance by now."

"She couldn't have gotten that far; it's only been a few hours."

"You clearly don't know her that well."

Chapter 92

Natalya was sitting in Todd's office, tapping her fingers on his desk impatiently. She had just given Todd a written statement about what she knew involving Seri, his business, and Brown. She couldn't stop thinking about what would happen to her if she was found out. She knew that Todd had offered to put her into Witness Protection, but what if Seri were to find out what she'd done before Todd could deliver.

She was going crazy, just sitting there. She remembered seeing Todd shut a desk drawer when she walked in, the bottom one. She went around the desk, pulled it open, and smiled. Scotch wasn't her drink of choice, but hell, right now, she'd drink anything. She poured a drink and turned her attention to the shelves against the wall, where he kept all his awards and pictures of his family.

She smiled when she saw the picture of Todd and his little girl. It brought back memories from her childhood when she herself was a sweet and innocent daddy's girl. Back to a time where the only thing that made her happy was being with her father. She was fighting back the tears when the thoughts of her father turned to a much darker place. Her eyes were red and watering when Todd came back into his office.

"How's it coming?" she asked.

"These things take time. I've given your statement to the District Attorney. He'll need to talk to you before any deal can be set," Todd said.

"You promised me protection. You said all I had to do was tell you what I knew, and I'd be protected."

"And you will be. But before that can happen, we need to make sure all of our ducks are in a row," Todd explained. "Are you sure everything you told me is accurate?"

"If I wrote it down, you can guarantee it happened. I've been around Seri for over 20 years. I've heard things I was meant to, and things I wasn't meant to."

"The biggest concern that the D.A. will have is trying to prove that it actually happened."

"I know people that will testify to every crime."

"And why didn't you name those people?" Todd asked.

"Get me in protection first, and I will give you a name for crimes you don't even know about," Natalya replied.

"What about Brown's team?" Todd asked.

"What about them? I'm giving you a major crime boss, and you're worried about those errand boys?"

"You of all people should know what they're capable of. They can be just as dangerous as Sokolov, if not more. Trust me on that."

"Really now?" Natalya asked. "What exactly do you know that I don't?"

"Let's just say that we have a history, a very personal history."

Chapter 93

"Captain Todd, how are you?" Mayor Sullivan asked as he entered the room.

"Mr. Mayor, thank you for coming in on such short notice."

"What's this about?"

"Mr. Sullivan, this is Natalya, a former associate to Seri Sokolov," Todd said.

"Well, I didn't expect that," Sullivan said as he turned his attention to Natalya. "What can I do for you, ma'am?"

"You can protect me. As I told the captain, Seri is losing control. He's making decisions without thinking them through, and now, I fear he's going to kill me," Natalya explained.

"I've offered her Witness Protection in exchange for her knowledge of Sokolov's operation, including Brown and his team," Todd said.

"Don't you think we should see what she knows before you start making promises you may not be able to keep?" Sullivan asked.

"Sir, with all due respect, this is too big of a fish to throw back. I believe it's worth the risk."

"How do we know you're telling the truth?" Sullivan asked, turning back to Natalya. "You could be playing us."

"I've given my statement to Todd with information on cases I know to be unsolved."

"And how do you know that?"

"Because I'm sitting here and not rotting in a jail cell," Natalya replied.

"You gave a statement incriminating yourself in an unsolved crime?"

"A murder to be more precise," Natalya said.

"You're admitting to a murder?" Sullivan asked.

"If that doesn't show you she's serious, sir, I don't know what will," Todd added.

Sullivan rubbed his chin for a second while he weighed his options. Todd was right; this was a big fish that was on the line, and if Natalya's statement turns out to be true, who knows what information she could give.

"All right, we'll have to make sure everything checks out before we can put you into Witness Protection."

"It already has," Todd said. "I pulled the file before I called you. Everything adds up."

"Okay, I'll start the paperwork and get everything in order. However, if anything that you tell us turns out to be false, I will bring the full weight of the law down on you," Sullivan said.

Natalya didn't say anything. She just stared at the ground, thinking. Her nerves had already been fried, and she was still scared. She finally looked up at the mayor and nodded. She knew the risks she was taking, and she was ready to just disappear. She was ready to start a new life in whatever small town she was sent to. There was just one problem.

"What do we do about Seri?"

Chapter 94

"I've been thinking about that, and I have a plan," Todd said as he took a seat behind his desk.

"What would that be?"

"It's risky, and you're not going to like it," he said, looking at Natalya. "But it's going to bring Seri out of hiding, and we'll be waiting."

"What do I have to do?" Natalya asked.

"Call Seri, tell him to meet you at the same docks where all this started, where he lost control, where two of my best lost their lives."

"What if he says no?"

"If he wants you dead like you're claiming, there's no way he'll turn you down," Sullivan said.

"And you'll be there to make sure I survive this meeting?"

"You have our word," Sullivan reassured her.

"Do you have any way of contacting anyone from Brown's team?" Todd asked.

"I have no idea," Natalya said, almost dumbfounded. "I might have an old contact number stored away."

"What are you getting at?" Sullivan asked.

"His body was never recovered; you said so yourself," Todd started. "Now, either we didn't look hard enough, or his guys got him out of there, and he could still be alive."

"There's absolutely no way that could even be possible," the mayor objected. "Even if his guys got him out of there, your report says that Sokolov shot him in the back at point-blank range."

"That's correct."

"He would've either hit the spine, paralyzing him no doubt. Or it would've trashed his organs, causing massive bleeding. Either way, he doesn't survive without immediate medical attention," Sullivan said.

"When Seri was shoving me into the car to leave, I saw one of them pushing and pulling the other two into a car and speeding off just before your backup arrived," Natalya added.

"And we know that they didn't go to any hospital in any burrow. There were checkpoints set up within an hour so they couldn't have gotten far," Sullivan started. "Even if he survived, and that's a big if, we would've found them no matter how good they are."

Todd sat at his desk just listening to the mayor talk to him like he was a child, pointing out all the ways he was wrong and how he just needed to forget about everything and focus on Sokolov. Which would be a great collar; no one would ever deny that. It just wasn't the one he wanted.

"We move on Sokolov and put him down. Natalya, I need you to make the call. Stay calm and convince him to meet you."

"I know that Brian is still alive," Todd said with almost a look of defeat on his face. At this point, everything that he had been trying to keep in the dark just kept busting out into the light.

"And how in the hell do you know that?" Sullivan asked.

"Because if he had actually died, his family would have had some kind of service, and his mother would have made sure I was there," Todd explained.

"Excuse me?" the mayor asked with growing confusion.

"I may have been closer to them than I let on, sir."

Chapter 95

It was finally out. Todd had just revealed that he had a personal connection with not just Brown but possibly the family. His career was basically over, so what else did he have to lose? He might as well just come clean and let the pieces fall where they may. At the very least, there was a chance he'd get the satisfaction of seeing the family in shambles and the bad guys behind bars where they belong.

"So, not only did you grow up with them, but you were part of the inner circle?" Sullivan asked, still processing what he had just heard.

"Now you can see why this is so personal for me."

"How could you not tell anyone about this?"

"And have every single decision I've ever made questioned? Have my whole career questioned?"

"That's already happening. Ever since your stunt at the docks, you've been under a microscope," Sullivan said. "You need to tell me everything."

"You already know everything. All the unsolved cases I have ever suspected them of being involved in, all the addresses they could've lived at. Everything is in his file," Todd said.

"What about your undercover operation with Tayler?" Sullivan asked. "There was very little paperwork on that."

"When we were younger, the Sokolov family had always been hanging around a dive bar not far from where we lived. I figured, why not take a look. I checked out the place, but it'd been abandoned," Todd explained. "I felt I was on to something, so I stayed with it. It took a couple of weeks, but eventually, I got lucky and spotted them heading into a bar off Vanderbilt, called Woodwork."

"They've been going there for years," Natalya added. "I've even been there when Seri held a couple of meetings."

"That's what I thought. So I sent Tayler in there as a waitress and just waited for one of them to take an interest in her."

"Okay, that all makes sense, but what it doesn't explain is where they are now and if Brian is, in fact, alive," Sullivan said, trying to piece it all together.

"We were a group of five. We did some dumb stuff when we were young, but when we were in our junior year, we caught Senior's attention. That's when I backed off," Todd said.

"I remember when those guys first started coming around. There was no fear. They acted like they belonged there," Natalya added. "Senior took a shine to them, and it wasn't long until Zack was offering his opinions, running some errands, and even sitting in on meetings."

"Something that Seri couldn't have liked," Todd said.

"Seri has hated Zack and his guys since the day they showed up. The only reason he kept him around is that he's been useful to him," Natalya said. Her side of the situation was already putting things into perspective.

"A few years back, Brian suddenly disappeared. Rumor on the street was that he died on the job," Todd continued.

"I remember that," Natalya added. "Zack said that they were shot at as they drove away, and one of the stray bullets caught Brian in the chest."

"That's not really hard to believe," Sullivan said. "I'm surprised it hadn't happened sooner."

"It's plausible, yeah, but not likely," Todd said.

"Why do you think that?"

"There's no way that Zack would've let that go. He would've been out for blood and wouldn't have stopped until he got revenge. He would've killed the shooters family in front of him before ripping him apart piece by piece," Todd explained.

"That's true. He would've been on the attack until the man who killed his friend was dead," Natalya added.

"How do you know he didn't?" Sullivan questioned. "If he's as good as you say he is, he would've had no problem staying under your radar."

"Because I checked. In the days after Brian's disappearance, there were no reported murders, no missing persons, not even reports of muggings anywhere," Todd explained.

"He's right," Natalya chimed in. "I remember the job, some low-level enforcer who was getting too comfortable in Seri's territory, so he sent them to dispose of him. When they got back, Zack didn't say much, he was pretty wrecked over Brian, but as Todd said, they never went after anyone."

"I know Brian's still alive," Todd said.

"Even if he is, there's no way to know for sure that they would have gone to him for help," Sullivan said.

"I found a contact number," Natalya said as she leaned against the window, looking at her phone.

"For Brown?"

"I don't know for sure; it's a burner phone that they keep with them in case of an emergency."

"Call it. If one of them answers, we can trace it," Sullivan ordered. "Put it on speaker. No offense, but I'm not going to risk us not hearing the entire conversation."

Chapter 96

I was in the bathroom, checking out my wounds in the mirror. They were healing well, and it was getting easier to move around. Still a little bit sore, but I wasn't complaining. I put my shirt back on and headed back into the kitchen where the guys had a map on the table that had Seri's loft, two of his safe houses, his favorite watering hole, and the most common routes he uses all highlighted.

"Are we sure he hasn't changed anything in his routine?" Brian asked.

"Why would he? As far as he's concerned, he's got nothing to worry about," Tony answered.

"What about Natano's crew?"

"That's the wild card we have to look out for," I said. "If they haven't taken any shots at him yet, it's a sure bet they're going to."

"How do we prepare for that?" Brian asked.

"We keep our eyes open. We can't afford to get tunnel vision on this. We've only got one shot," John said. "We know all the major players in Natano's crew; if we see any of them, we back off."

"What if they use someone new?" Tony asked.

"They wouldn't; this is too personal now. They wouldn't risk a newbie messing up a hit on someone like Seri," I answered.

I was looking at the map, just playing out a few scenarios in my head. The easiest way was obviously just to ambush him at his loft. The four of us bust in and just start shooting, but that would leave so many loose ends. Even using silencers, there's still the risk of neighbors hearing the commotion, seeing us in the hallway, or even spotting us outside. And all that's just assuming he was at home alone.

That's when I remembered his car, a jet-black Escalade with limo tint on all the windows. Maybe one night, when he was at the bar knocking back shots of vodka with his bodyguard and driver, we move. Brian could be inside the bar keeping an eye on everything, while John and Tony wait by the door outside, I could break into Seri's car and wait.

When they came out of the bar, John could come up behind the three stumbling men and use a stun gun to take care of the driver while slipping a knife into the kidney of his bodyguard. Once Seri went for his gun, Tony could step in and apply his patent "rear-naked chokehold" that he'd mastered from many nights watching *WWE Monday Night Raw*. Once Seri had passed out, they'd load him into the car, and we'd be on our way. I was looking at possible escape routes, and just as I was starting to get it all in line, a phone started ringing.

"It's not mine," I said.

"It's the burner. I kept it charged up just in case we needed a favor," John said as he pulled it out of his pocket. "Son of a bitch."

"What?" I asked.

"Son of a bitch," Tony said as John showed them the caller ID.

"What the hell does that crazy bitch want?" Brian asked.

"Let's find out," I said as I motioned for John to flip open the phone.

Chapter 97

"You've got a set of balls calling us," John said. "What do you want?"

"John? Is that you?"

"Seeing how you dialed this number, you know damn well who you're talking to," John said, raising his voice.

"There's that Irish temper I know and love."

"What the hell do you want, Natalya?" John asked again as I motioned him to put the call on speaker.

"I want you guys to leave me alone, for good."

"And why would we do that? Your boyfriend tried to kill us."

"Ex-boyfriend, and he wants me dead too."

"Well, so do we. You've caused us a hell of a lot of problems."

"I'm aware. I also know better than to call and ask for a favor without having something bigger to offer."

"You're gonna bribe me? That's hilarious. What could you possibly have that would make me not want to hunt you down?"

"What I have isn't for you, it's for Zack," Natalya said. She was taking a huge risk. She wasn't sure if Todd's assumption was true or not, but, at this point, she didn't have anything to lose.

"Excuse me?" John asked in shock. All four of us were surprised. If she knew I was still alive, did Seri? Was she trying to get them to make an emotional response? Or was she just trying to get a reaction out of us?

"I said what I have to offer is for Zack," she repeated. "He is sitting with you, isn't he? And if he gives an order, you follow it just like the trained puppy you are."

"Yeah, I'm here," I said, cutting John off. Knowing his temper, he was about to explode, and based on the look he was giving me, I was going to be the one that suffered his wrath. "Now, what do you have to offer?"

"Seri."

"You're offering up Seri?" I asked. "Now, why am I skeptical about that?"

"Yeah, I knew you would be."

"So, what's the plan? Call me and lure me out by offering Seri, and then what? He finishes what he started at the docks?"

"No, quite the opposite actually, I lure him out, and you do what he couldn't. You kill that son of a bitch before he gets a chance to finish you."

"Well, as tempting as that sounds, I'm gonna have to pass."

"Pass?" Natalya repeated. "I'm offering you the one person you want dead more than anyone, the man that you believe is responsible for Senior's death, and you're gonna pass?"

"Yeah, you see, if there is anyone who I trust less than Seri, it would be you. And the last thing I would ever do is take your word on anything. If you say Seri wants you dead, then so be it—you just better hope I get to him before he gets to you."

"You're signing my death warrant," Natalya said.

"Ten years too late," I answered. "But there is one thing I have to ask."

"What?" Natalya asked, holding back tears.

"How did you know I wasn't dead?"

"I didn't. It was a bluff. I was hoping that I could play on your weakness for girls in need. I guess Seri has rubbed off on you more than you let on," Natalya said as she hung up the phone and stared at Sullivan.

Chapter 98

"Well played," Sullivan said as he stared at Natalya. "How did you know they were together?"

"I didn't, but I took a chance. It seemed like the only card that I had to play, and it looks like it paid off."

"In a huge way," Todd said as he came back into the room. "We were able to ping the cell signal off a tower in Portland, Maine."

"Were you able to get an exact location?"

"No, but I have a pretty good idea where they've been hiding."

"Where?" Sullivan asked.

"When we were kids, Brian had family up in Portland, a grandmother, I believe. I'm willing to bet that's where they're at," Todd explained.

"So, let's go get them," Natalya said.

"It's not that simple," Sullivan said.

"Even if it were, by the time we would be able to get anyone there, they'd be long gone. Probably already packing and leaving now," Todd added.

"So what do we do? Sit here and watch as he and Seri just disappear?"

"No, we keep the same plan," Sullivan said. "We use Seri to bring out Brown, or vice versa."

"With all due respect, sir, Zack isn't going to fall into a trap like that. After what happened at the docks, he's going to be extra cautious," Todd said.

"That's why we don't set a trap. We manipulate him. How much of a weakness is a damsel in distress?" Sullivan asked.

"As far back as I can remember, he's always tried to be the *'go-to-guy'* when it came to girls. When we were little, he wanted to be the one they called on when they had problems they needed to solve. Needless to say, he's been kicking in teeth for a very long time, even if it wasn't deserved," Todd explained.

"So we play that angle. We give it a day or two while we tail Sokolov. Let's get familiar with his day-to-day activities, and then when the time is right, we send a distress text," Sullivan said.

"A distress text?" Natalya asked.

"It's safe to assume that Brown and his guys are on the hunt for Sokolov and that they'll stop at nothing until he's dead. Now regardless of his hatred for you, there's no way that he'd let a piece of shit like Seri kill a woman," Sullivan explained.

"And if we know where Seri is, we can know the perfect time to send that text," Todd said, finishing Sullivan's thought. "Natalya, we can manipulate Brown into coming to rescue you and take them both down."

"Do you think he'll go for it?"

"If what you two have told me turns out to be true, it's worth the risk. At the very least, we'll get Sokolov, and that is a win no matter how you look at it," Sullivan said.

Chapter 99

"So what the fuck do we do now?" John asked.

"She doesn't know anything, let's just relax," I said, trying to remain calm.

"Relax?" John repeated. "Zacky, we were holding all the cards before you said anything. What the hell were you thinking?"

"Because if I didn't, she would've played on your anger, and you would've done something stupid," I said, pointing at him.

"Get your goddamn finger out of my face before I break it off."

"Take your best shot," I said as I stood up. Thankfully, Tony and Brian stepped in. I'm in no condition to fight, but I wasn't going to let them see that.

"Guys, seriously? We've got too much at stake here for you two to start unraveling now," Tony said as he put himself between John and me. "Both of you sit down and shut the hell up."

"Tony's right, guys, we don't need this right now. We've gotta stay focused," Brian said. "We've gotta treat this like any of the high profile jobs we've done in the past. That means leaving the emotion out of it."

"You're right, B, you're right," I said as I stuck my hand out toward John as a truce. "No sense in us going at this one guy down."

"Oh, you're such a dick," John said as he shook my hand with a smile. "What's our next move?"

"We stay the course," Brian said. "Natalya knows we're going to be coming for Seri, and she tried asking us for help, right? So let's assume we're not the only people she'd turn to."

"Who else would she go to?" Tony asked. "It's not like she has a lot of people close to her."

"There's really no way to be sure. But if we turned her down, I wouldn't be surprised at anything she does next," John said.

"Why wouldn't she just disappear?"

"She's scared," I said. "Her whole life, she's been able to manipulate her way into getting anything she's wanted. Now all of a sudden, she has nowhere to run and nowhere to hide."

"Well, that may be true, but we still need to keep her in mind. As John said, she could do anything now," Tony added.

That was one thing I honestly hadn't taken into consideration. I had just assumed that when we caught up to Seri, she'd just end up being collateral damage. Now she was reaching out to me for help.

Chapter 100

Natalya sat in what had to be the most uncomfortable chair that had ever been made, as she waited for Todd and Mayor Sullivan to return with all the necessary paperwork that would officially make her a rat.

"Is this what my life has come to?" she said as she stared blankly at the tile floor.

"Not a month ago, I had it all, and now what? I'm running from a spineless piece of trash, and I'm so desperate I came to the cops for help," she continued. "I'm a disgrace."

Natalya hadn't felt so helpless since she was a child fighting to get away from her abusive parents. She had finally won that battle and disappeared, and, at the time, she thought that there was nothing in the world that could ever bring her back down. She even smiled when she received word that her father had finally passed. That was probably the best news she'd ever heard. Now she was just as scared as she'd been when hiding under her bed, hoping that her drunken father would just leave her alone for one night. The walls were crashing in when Todd came back through the door, snapping her out of her own personal nightmare.

"Okay, we're just about set," he said. "By this time tomorrow, you'll be a confidential informant, and no one outside this office will know your involvement."

"All I have to do is sign the paper?" she asked.

"Well, yes and no," Todd answered.

"And just what the fuck does that mean?"

"You have given us some very reliable intel along with some very farfetched stories."

"You think I'm lying?"

"No. Personally, I think you downplayed some of it. But the higher-ups don't like to believe such a thing could happen in their city without them knowing about it and putting a stop to it."

"So, what do I need to do?" Natalya questioned. "What hoops are you going to make me jump through now?"

"I wouldn't call them hoops," Sullivan said as he came into the room. "I would call it being prepared for the worst."

Sullivan took a seat behind Todd's desk as he measured Natalya up. You could tell by the look on his face that he still wasn't sure if this was real or a trap.

"And what does being prepared for the worst involve?" she asked as she turned her attention to the mayor.

"Nothing more than what we've already discussed."

"I don't know," Natalya said, shaking her head. "Your entire plan is based on your men being able to get the best of Seri *and* Zack. With all due respect, that's not a big confidence booster."

"Yeah, that is true. However, this time, we have you, and that, my dear, can go a long way."

"All right, fine. What do we do?"

"We put you back out on the street, with an undercover detail, of course, and we'll use your phone to text Seri and just wait for him to come to you," Sullivan said.

"You think he's dumb enough to walk into a trap?"

"Maybe he is, maybe he's not," Todd said. "But emotions do crazy things to people. When he finally sees you, those emotions could get the better of him, and he'll go straight at you. That's when we move in."

"I hope you guys are faster than he is. Because when he sees me, he isn't going to yell, scream, or even take a swing. He's just going to simply pull up and shoot," Natalya explained.

"We will be there to make sure that doesn't happen. You have my word. I will not let that sack of shit hurt you," Todd said.

"When do we start?" she asked with her hands shaking.

"First thing in the morning," Sullivan answered.

Chapter 101

The NYPD has a few safe houses around the city. Some of which are in nice hotels that are mainly for the investment types that are testifying against Wall Street tycoons for the SEC and some are barely houses at all. The ones that they save for the junkies and rats that have double-crossed their bosses were just basically slum housing. Leaky roofs, broken windows, rotted floors, no air, no heat, all accompanied with roaches that were bigger than some dogs.

Unfortunately for Natalya, Todd and Sullivan had dropped her off at the least desirable option. She scanned the room, looking for a spot that didn't repulse her so she could at least sit down. There was an old couch in the middle of the room, probably the same couch that had been there when the house was built back in the 60s. The green, cream-colored couch was pointed at a TV next to the wall to her left and behind the couch was a dining table that sat four. Two of the chairs looked to have holes in the cushion, most likely made by rats, and oddly enough, the other two looked to be in perfect condition.

The kitchen was barely big enough to even open the oven door. That wasn't really a problem; she wasn't much of a cook. She wasn't even sure why she was here. She really had nowhere to go, nowhere to run. Sullivan was being way too over cautious for her liking. He had even assigned two officers to stay with her in the house overnight. There was nothing she could do about that, so she was trying to make her peace with it.

"You don't have to worry, Miss. You're in good hands," one of the officers said as he turned on the light to the only bedroom. "We're going to be here in the living room all night."

"My heroes," Natalya replied as she walked into the bedroom and shut the door.

She looked around the room while she took off her jacket and tossed it on the bed. As bad as the house was, the bedroom was actually well maintained, and there was a clean smell to it. The sheets appeared to be fresh, and the floor vacuumed. She turned around and dropped down onto the bed. She stared at the wall, trying to pull herself together, but her nerves were starting to get the best of her. The same thought kept racing through her head. *How was it all going to play out?*

She debated back and forth most of the night. Could she actually survive this whole thing? Of course she could. She'd gone through worse and survived. She believed that Todd could really get her out of this. He had drawn up a great plan. All he had to do was execute it. But *could* he?

On the flip side of the coin, what if Seri got to her first? What would happen then? The obvious answer would be that he would kill her. But what if he didn't? What if he decided to keep her alive for a little while longer? Her eyes were starting to water when one of the officers knocked on the door.

"Ma'am, can we get you anything? Are you hungry or thirsty?"

"I'm fine," she said, wiping away a tear. "I'm just going to get some sleep. I have a big day tomorrow."

Chapter 102

Natalya didn't sleep at all. She spent most of the night just staring out the window. For all she knew, this could be the last sunrise she'd ever see. The way the bricks of the building next door lit up under the sunlight brought a half-smile to her face. That was the best look at it she was going to get, and she was fine with that.

The smell of coffee started to make its way under the door, and before long, it overtook the entire room. She could hear the two officers talking to each other from the kitchen. From what she could make out, it was a heated debate about who had the better chance to make the playoffs—the Giants or the Jets.

"Boys and their sports," she said as she put on her jacket and opened the bedroom door.

The two officers quickly lowered their voices, and one poked his head out of the kitchen to make sure Natalya wasn't making a run for it.

"We didn't wake you, did we?"

"In order to wake someone, one must first be asleep," Natalya replied.

"Rough night, huh? I guess that's to be expected," he started. "Not to overstep, but you've got to have a million different emotions right now."

Natalya smirked, pulled out a chair, and took a seat before she asked, "What's your name?"

"Ross."

"Well, Ross, you cannot begin to imagine what I've gone through. I don't mean to be rude, but don't try to understand what's going on."

"My apologies, ma'am."

The two sat in silence at the table while the other officer stayed in the kitchen with nothing but the sound of coffee being slurped to break the silence. After a few minutes, Ross received a text message saying that Todd was outside, waiting.

This was it. All the things that have happened in her life, all the close calls, all the abuse, everything came down to this. Her life could be over within a few hours, but she couldn't focus on that. She was doing everything she could to put her faith in Todd and his plan—even if she wasn't convinced it would work.

"How was your night?" Todd asked as Natalya and the two officers made their way down the stairs to the back alley.

"Just like I was at the *Four Seasons,*" Natalya answered with sarcasm.

"I apologize. I know it's not the typical accommodation that you are used to, but, truth be told, that's one of the reasons you made it through the night," Todd explained.

"I'm aware. I don't mean to be ungrateful; it was just a long night."

"I understand," Todd said as he nodded his head and opened the door for his frazzled informant. As he went around to the driver's side, he ordered the two officers to head back to headquarters and check in with Mayor Sullivan. As he got behind the wheel, he could sense how uneasy Natalya was. Understandable, no doubt, but he still felt it was his responsibility to try and calm her nerves.

"This is a good plan," he said.

"I know you think that; I just know that there are factors that no plan can predict," Natalya answered. "I'm sure you have your best people on it, I'm just nervous."

The two of them drove in silence for a few blocks in stop-and-go New York City traffic. As they waited for a light to turn green, Natalya started to recognize a few of the buildings, and her heart sank.

"Where are we going?"

"We are going to tail Seri; I need you with me to point out any and all people that could interfere with our operation," Todd replied.

"The only one I can think that would even be a problem would be Seri's personal bodyguard, Ivan," Natalya said.

"Well, just to be safe, let's follow him for a little bit."

Chapter 103

It was lunch hour in the city when Brian and I started from Seri's loft and followed a route that we determined would be the main one he would use. We were on foot, so it would be easier to see into restaurants and pubs we passed, but so far nothing. I knew we weren't going to see him in the first place we started, but I was impatient. I wanted to get this done before things got even more out of control.

"Oh, come on," I said in frustration. "Where the hell is this son of a bitch?"

"Patience, brother, patience," Brian answered. "We'll find him."

We kept looking. We even took a couple of side streets just in case luck was on our side. It wasn't, at least not to this point. We had looked in every window, alley, parked car for a solid 20 blocks, and we had nothing to show for it. I took a seat on a bench and rubbed my temples, trying to fight off a headache, but it was a losing battle. I have never been the most patient person in the world, and this *hide and seek* game was not helping. This wasn't like anything else we'd done before. It was always precise timing to everything; we knew all scenarios and had backup plans for our backup plans. But this, this was infuriating. Then, as if from out of nowhere, lady luck smiled on us.

"Hey, does that car look familiar?" Brian asked, pointing to an SUV that had just pulled up to a stop sign.

"Well, would you look at that?" I said with a smile. "Good things do happen to good people."

There it was, plain as day. An Escalade with limo tint on the windows, I'd know that car anywhere. I watched as the car made a right turn and headed toward us. I tucked my head down, and Brian turned his back to the road to avoid being seen. As the Escalade passed, I looked up to watch it make a left and then turn into a parking garage across a shopping center. We were just about to cross the street and head to the decorative water fountain that was in front of the mall when I noticed another car. A pearl white Camry that had come from the same intersection the Escalade had come from.

"Are you fucking kidding me?"

"Call Tony. Get them down here now."

Chapter 104

"You have to stop being nervous," Todd said as he and Natalya sat in his unmarked car, waiting.

"Seriously? You must work on your pep talks. You suck at them."

"Look behind us."

"Why?" Natalya wondered.

"Humor me, please? What do you see?"

"People walking in and out of coffee shops, not even bothering to look up from their phones. Taxi cabs, traffic. What am I looking for?"

"You see that car, silver Impala, about four cars back on the other side of the street?"

"What about it?"

"That's backup. They have been with us since I picked you up this morning," Todd explained. "They are here to make sure nothing happens to you."

"There's only two of them?"

"So? It's just a surveillance op. We're not going to do anything crazy today; this is just to learn his habits."

Natalya didn't respond; she just kept tapping her coffee cup and staring at the building to her right. The people that passed by on the sidewalk didn't even seem to have faces—they were basically ghosts. Her own mother could be standing outside that window, and she wouldn't have even noticed. The past three days, she maybe had slept for a total of six hours; she was out of it. She reached down to adjust her seat, and when it was laid back just far enough, she closed her eyes. Thoughts were flying through her mind, and the harder she tried to shut them down, the more they persisted. Just as she started to fall asleep, there was a sharp and short honk of a horn.

"What was that?" she asked, rubbing her eyes.

"That, my dear, was a signal. Do you recognize the car about to pass?"

"That's him," Natalya said.

"Are you sure?"

"Never been more certain of anything in my life."

That was good enough for Todd. He threw the car into drive and started following the car that they had been waiting to see. They tried to stay, at minimum, four car links behind. The car they were tailing was making random turns, obviously trying to lose all tails, but Todd was one of the best pursuit drivers the department had ever seen. There was no way he was going to let that Escalade out of his sight, not even for a moment.

Traffic was surprisingly light given the time of day, which made it a little more difficult to keep the distance Todd felt comfortable with, but he was still confident that he could keep from being seen. They had managed to stay with the black SUV despite the dozen or so turns it had made as precautions. Todd had used a tactic he had dubbed *"stop and go."* He thought that if you acted like any other car in traffic, the less chance you had of being made. He would get up to the speed limit and be only a car link away, and then he'd be slow to leave an intersection, giving the Escalade a head start, so to speak.

Natalya knew the area they were in. They weren't far from the loft, maybe 20 minutes or so, and when she saw the beautiful statue that stood in a water fountain outside a shopping mall, she knew exactly where they were going.

"I know this place," she said as Todd waited for the light to change.

"How's that?"

"Seri brought me here a few times to buy me a necklace or a new outfit— basically anything that he thought would keep me quiet."

"Keep you quiet?"

"Usually, before we went inside, Seri would meet with people he called 'friends' up on the third floor of the parking garage."

"Is that where he's going?" Todd asked.

"It would be my guess."

"Hall? You there?" Todd said into his walkie talkie.

"Go for Hall."

"We believe he's going to the third floor. You guys park on four and come down the stairs. Be on your toes."

Chapter 105

Brian and I walked into the parking garage just as a silver Impala roared up the ramp toward the second floor. We were stuck with the stairs. They were going to be faster than the elevator; anyone that's ever been in a parking garage would know that. As we were about halfway up the stairs, Brian reached back and handed me a gun with a homemade silencer on it. We were making our way up the stairwell as fast and as quietly as we could, and just as we reached the third-floor door, we heard a door above us open and slam shut.

"What do we do?" Brian asked as the echo of footsteps rushed down the stairs toward us.

"We finish this by any means necessary," I said as I pointed my gun at the top of the stairs.

As the footsteps got louder, I took a couple of deep breaths and kept my gun pointed at the blind corner. I couldn't help but feel a little sorry for the poor bastards running down the stairs. They didn't know what they were about to stumble on, but as life has cruelly taught me, sometimes you're just at the wrong place at the wrong time. Two men came around the corner, and I don't even think they saw us. After four shots, two in each chest, their lifeless bodies tumbled down the rest of the stairs until they stopped at our feet.

"Just like riding a bike, huh?" I asked Brian.

He didn't respond; he just bent down and started going through the pockets of the two men. Outside of a camera, I didn't see anything, but Brian was what you might call a perfectionist. He was going to make sure there was no wallet, no card, cash, I.D., anything. Right as I was about to pull open the door to the third floor, he called me.

"Hey, check this out."

"What do you have?"

"A shield," Brian said as he pulled an NYPD badge out from under the shirt of one of the dead stair runners.

"Well, if one was a cop, it's a safe assumption," I said as Brian pulled out the second man's badge.

"Okay, so that was Todd in the car?" I asked as I let the door close behind me. "I knew it, I fucking knew it."

"Calm down, Zacky. This is good news."

"Good news?" I repeated in disbelief.

"If these guys are cops, that means Todd is close, and if Todd is close, we can end everything. We can be completely out. Two birds, one stone."

"No," I objected. "We do not move on Todd unless he gives us absolutely no choice. Do you hear me?"

"Understood," Brian said.

"Where are Tony and John?"

"They should be pulling up any minute now."

"Have them get to the third floor ASAP. Tell them to find the car."

I nodded at Brian, and we both caught our breath before slowly pulling open the door. I went first and snuck behind a cherry red Dodge Ram truck while Brian let the door shut with as little noise as possible. He caught up to me, and together we moved one car at a time. After the Dodge, we ducked behind a neon green 350Z, next was a funky gold Explorer, and just before we moved again, I grabbed Brian's arm and pulled him in toward me.

"There's Todd."

Chapter 106

"Okay, this is perfect," Todd said.

"How do you figure that?"

"Look, it's only Seri and his driver," Todd pointed out. "This is the best time to text him and get him to come to us."

"I don't know. Something seems off," Natalya answered.

"I'll call Hall and have them meet us here with all the weapons they can carry. When Seri gets here, he won't know what hit him," Todd said, trying to convince Natalya.

"Okay, let's do it."

Natalya pulled out her phone, flipped it open, and started to write out the text. As she used her imagination to make it sound as believable as possible, she couldn't help overhearing Todd trying to reach his people. There wasn't an answer; she didn't think too much of it, they were in a garage, they probably turned down the volume so nobody would hear them. But then the second, third, and fourth time that there wasn't an answer, that's when she began to panic.

"What's going on?" she asked.

"It's a garage. Radios rarely work here," Todd answered. That wasn't the answer she wanted, but it was enough to keep her going—she finally hit send.

Seri, I'm here. I'm on the 3rd floor, waiting on you to come for me. Let's end this.

"It's sent; he should be here in no time. Will your people be ready?"

"They'll be ready. You just need to be out of sight when he gets here," Todd said as he got out of the car.

That was the best plan Natalya had heard in months. She didn't want to be anywhere near Seri when all this went down. She looked at Todd, who was crouching down at the stairs that led to the entrance of the strip mall, waiting for Seri to start his climb up. She heard a bottle get kicked along the concrete of the garage, and oddly enough, it made her smile' it was Todd's backup. He had come through, and he would get her out of this. She reached to the side of her seat and laid it back as far as it could go. She finally felt like she could sleep now. She closed her eyes and started drifting off when she heard a familiar voice.

"Well, hey, sweetheart."

"John?"

Chapter 107

Brian and I had started coming up to a line of cars, and from our vantage point, we could see John and Tony standing behind the Camry we'd seen following Seri, and in front of that, I could see our old friend Todd taking cover in the corner next to the stairs with a BMW blocking his view of us. Brian and I crouched down and hurried over to John, who had pulled Natalya out of the car with his hand grasped over her mouth to keep her quiet. He was able to overpower her and pin her to the wall.

"Well, hello, darling, how are you?" I asked as the four of us surrounded her.

"What do you want?" Natalya whispered.

"Why is Todd here?" John asked. Natalya didn't answer. Instead, she just looked up at us with a blank stare.

"Don't make me smack you," Tony said.

"I'm going to ask you one more time. If you don't answer, I'm going to let my boys have their fun," I said as I grabbed her by the throat. "Why is Todd here?"

Natalya still didn't answer. I'll give it to her—she's a tough bitch, not the smartest but tough nevertheless. I kept my hand on her throat and squeezed but still, no answer. I tightened my grip and started to pick her up when she finally coughed and spit it out.

"He's here for Seri."

"Seri's here?" Brian asked. "Where?"

"On his way to the car," Natalya was able to cough out.

"See what I mean, good things…" I said with a smile. Everything was falling into place. We were able to find Seri and follow him not only without him knowing, but we even managed to not be seen by Todd. His obsession with catching us had apparently given him tunnel vision, but as they say, sometimes it's better to be lucky than good.

"You're not wrong, boss," Brian said as he pointed to the stairwell. Ivan had already made his way into the garage from the steps, and Seri wasn't too far behind him. They were walking like madmen toward the row of cars, both with a gun in hand. They looked into a navy-blue Ford Ranger, nothing. Then it was a red Chevy Cavalier, again nothing. Then they turned their attention to the Camry, and just as Ivan reached for the driver's side door, Todd made his move.

"Hands in the air!" he shouted as he approached Seri from behind. Before the echo had time to repeat his command, Ivan and Seri had turned and pointed their guns at Todd.

"I wouldn't do that if I were you," Todd said. "I'm not alone."

"Looks like you are," Seri said.

"Hall, move in!" Todd shouted. "Hall, do you copy?"

"Now, that's a shame," Ivan said as he moved next to Seri. "You are in way over your head."

"So, you're who she ran to," Seri said, piecing it together. "Where is she?"

Chapter 108

This was turning into an explosive situation. Todd showed his hand too soon, he had no backup, and we had Natalya. Brian moved two spots down to the right of me and was behind a black four-door sedan. Tony went a few spots to my left and got between two cars and readied his gun. John still had a death grip on Natalya's waist with his left hand clasped over her mouth. He had maneuvered her behind a cement support pillar, and I was on the other side of the pillar between it and the hood of the white Camry.

"So, tell me, where is your so-called backup?" Seri asked.

"Oh, that's right, you don't have any," Ivan added.

"Don't make this worse than it already is," Todd started. "This doesn't have to go down like this. I can help you."

"Help me?" Seri asked with a grin. "In case you haven't noticed, I can take care of myself."

"Right, that's why you travel with a bodyguard."

"Hey! Watch your damn mouth!" Ivan shouted as he took a few steps at Todd.

I made eye contact with Tony, gave him a nod, and watched as he took aim at the back of Ivan's head. Then I got Brian's attention and signaled him to wait until my mark to move. Todd, ever the optimistic, kept trying to talk down the two Russians, just hoping that he had backup on the way. I was slightly impressed that he had lasted this long. Knowing Seri, I would've bet money that he would've shot him as soon as he saw him. As big of a pain in the ass as Todd was to me, magnify that by ten, and you might be close to how Seri felt about him.

As the three of them kept mouthing off back and forth, I knelt and started moving toward the trunk of the Camry to get a better view. After everything that had happened over the years, I still couldn't believe that I was still trying to save Todd. I should just let Seri shoot him and then move in, but honestly, I don't want to give him the satisfaction of taking out a high-ranking captain of the NYPD.

"This is your last chance. Put down your weapons and put your hands behind your head," Todd ordered. He had his gun trained on Seri's chest and hadn't broken eye contact with him. Seri took a couple of deep breaths and smiled.

"Okay, don't shoot. I'm going to put my gun down," Seri said as he held up his gun and slowly started to put it on the ground. As Seri lowered his weapon, Todd lowered his guard, only for a moment, but that's all it took. When Todd's attention was solely on Seri, Ivan took the shot.

I watched it happen, almost in slow motion. I could see Todd, not even bothering to look at Ivan. I saw the flash, hell I even saw the shell casing leave the gun, but I couldn't move. All I could do was watch as a bullet flew at Todd and strike him on his right side, just under the ribs. He went down like a sack of bricks, and before Seri could even stand back up to gloat, Tony fired a shot that landed dead center in Ivan's back.

"What that fuck?" Seri shouted as he turned to his bodyguard. He dropped to his knees and tried to do whatever he could to stop the bleeding, but it was no use. Tony was a great marksman and, even if Ivan managed to survive, he was going to be in a wheelchair for the rest of his life.

"Ivan, my friend, stay with me!" he said as he cradled his head in his lap and frantically tried to call for help.

"Talk about balance," I said as Tony, Brian, and I walked toward Seri with our guns drawn. "You shoot one of our friends; we shoot one of yours."

"You? You're supposed to be dead!"

"Well, I never did like doing what I was supposed to do."

"So, I guess this is how it ends?" Seri asked, looking at the ground without getting up.

"Only seems fair," Tony answered as he padded him down just to be sure he didn't have a second gun on him.

"What happened to Natalya?"

"You know, I'm gonna be honest with you. She called us, looking for help. She said you were going to kill her," I said as I sat down cross-legged in front of Seri.

"She wasn't wrong," he interrupted.

"I wanted to believe that she changed, I really did. But then, I remembered what my mom had always said when she talked about my father, '*A leopard can't change its spots.*'"

"What's your point?"

"You see, my father never changed, and I assumed that Natalya would never change, either. She was always out for herself, and when she offered you up, I knew something was off," I explained.

Seri just stared at me. It was like looking into a shark's eyes—there was no emotion. It was as if he was looking straight through me. I held my hand up and waved John over. He still had Natalya in his grasp, but by this point, she had stopped trying to fight. Her mascara was running, and her eyes were swollen, but there were no tears. She had finally seemed to make peace with what was about to happen.

"You see, I've been waiting for this ever since I put a handful of dirt onto Senior's casket," I said as I raised my gun. I waited till John pulled Natalya behind me and made the two of them lock eyes. A few moments passed, and then John tightened his grip on her chin and pulled as hard as he could until he felt the vertebras in her neck turn to dust.

"Goodbye, you piece of shit," I said as Seri screamed in Russian. He got out a few words and then, boom. His head snapped back and brain matter leaked from the back of his head as he fell to the ground.

Chapter 109

"Holy shit, you did it," Tony said. "I can't believe it, it's over. We're out."

I sat there looking at Seri's lifeless body. I had so many emotions running through my head. Honestly, I expected to see him jump back up and try and make a run for it. The man seemed to have nine lives. I just couldn't believe I was lucky enough to catch him when he was on life number nine.

"You okay?" Brian asked as he put his arm on my shoulder.

"Yeah, I'm good," I said as I picked myself up. I smiled as I pulled Brian in and hugged him. He started laughing as Tony and John came up and turned it into a group hug.

"Wow, what do we do now?" John asked.

"We get the hell out of here," Tony answered.

"Is Todd alive?" I asked. I looked over at him, and he wasn't moving. I started walking to him just to double-check, and that's when I saw his chest rising and falling.

"I'll call it in," John said as I knelt to check on him.

"You with us, Greg?"

"You…you're under arrest," he said, desperately trying to catch his breath.

"Yeah, I'm sure we are, buddy. Why don't you just relax, concentrate on breathing, and try not to die," Tony said as the guys came up to check on him.

"You have the right to remain silent," Todd continued.

"He's going into shock," Brian said. "How far out are the EMTs?"

"Minutes, probably closer," John said.

"All right, Greg, listen up. An ambulance will be here soon, okay?" I said as I squeezed his hand and started to stand up and walk away. That's when Todd squeezed back.

"I will find you," he said, staring straight into my eyes. "You will not get away."

Todd's grip loosened, and his hand fell to the concrete. He was still breathing—he was just unconscious. We could finally hear sirens in the distance as we started heading back up the stairs to John's car.

The four of us climbed into the car and made our exit to the streets. We passed a few squad cars, sirens blaring, followed closely by two ambulances. I kept staring out the window, just watching buildings pass. I didn't even realize we had made it out of the city. We were heading back to Brian's grandparents' place in Portland to lay low for a day or so. We were all silent; hell, to be honest, we were all lost in our own minds.

"Where do we go from here?" John asked again, still searching for an answer.

"I hear Dallas is nice this time of the year," Tony answered as he looked over at Brian.

"You know, I've been waiting for you guys to come visit for years," Brian said. "We have plenty of room for you guys."

"Tell you what? I'll meet you guys there," I said. "I just have one more thing I have to take care of."

Chapter 110

"Are you sure you don't want me to come in with you? You've had a rough couple of weeks."

"No, Mom, I'm fine. Really, I just want to be alone for a night."

"Okay, honey, I understand, but please call me if you need anything."

"I will. Love you, Mom."

"Love you too, sweetheart."

Tayler shut the passenger door of her mom's Jeep Cherokee, waved, and watched her drive away. She then turned and started limping her way up the stairs of her building. The walk to her apartment wasn't the easiest thing she'd ever done, but she was too proud to let anyone help her, let alone ask for help.

She finally got to her door, unlocked it, and staggered in. She turned to lock the door behind her, and as she flicked on the lamp that sat on her end table, she heard the distinct click of a gun hammer being pulled back.

She froze. After the gun battle and explosion that nearly took her life, she was in no shape to try and dodge a bullet. She slowly moved her hand from the light switch at the base of the lamp to under the table, looking for her backup weapon, but she couldn't feel it.

"Do you really think I didn't give this whole place a once over?" I asked.

"Zack? I thought you were dead."

"Surprise."

"How the fuck did you find me?"

"Well, darling, I'm kind of an expert at half-truths," I started as she turned around. "Take you, for instance, a rookie detective on her first undercover assignment. Now in my experience, cover identities are made to pass any background check."

"What's your point?"

"My point is that I'm willing to bet that your assignment, much like your late husband's, was given under false pretenses. Which means you wouldn't have gotten a deep cover alias, correct?"

"Still doesn't explain how you found me."

"The half-truths led me here, baby doll."

"Half-truths?"

"When we first met, you told me your name was Veronica; then, at my house, you said it was Tayler. It didn't even occur to me that you were telling me your last name. Then it hit me, put it together. Veronica Tayler."

"I'm impressed. Especially since you were able to access my files. They're confidential."

"You have your job, and I have mine," I said as I stood up. "Why don't you take a seat?"

"So why find me? You're presumed dead. You could've disappeared."

"Oh, don't worry about me, I'll be gone soon enough," I said as I sat on the coffee table in front of her. "I need you to give Todd a message for me."

I looked into her eyes as she sat in her recliner, frozen in fear. I moved the hair that hung down in front of her eye and tucked it behind her ear.

"I'm really sorry about this, but maybe, finally, he'll learn his lesson," I said as I rose my gun and fired one shot into her shoulder. The bullet went straight through her and the chair, coming to a stop in the cement wall that separated her living room from her bedroom. Tayler began to scream in agony and started to fall out of the chair before I caught her and repositioned her back in the recliner.

"What lesson is he supposed to learn from this?" she asked as she struggled to catch her breath.

"Don't hunt what you can't kill," I said as I stood up and started to leave. As I got to the door, I turned and fired one last shot that struck her above her left eye, and she went limp.

I grabbed a shirt that she was lying over the back of her couch and whipped all prints that I may have left behind. I tossed the gun on the couch and took my exit through the front door. I walked down the hallway to the stairs, where I passed a lovely older lady. We exchanged pleasantries, and after she passed me, I waited just for a minute. I heard her stop and knock on a door.

"Honey, you forgot your cell phone," she called out.

I heard a door squeak open, and after that, a blood-chilling scream. That was my cue to vanish. My job was finally done.